Plaguewalker

Gemma Tarlach

Printed in the United States of America

First Printing, 2012

ISBN: 0985260505
ISBN-13: 978-0-9852605-0-7

Grunaskhan Books

www.grunaskhanbooks.com

For Wiley

Acknowledgments

Writing is a solitary activity, but this book would not exist without the support and encouragement of others. My deepest thanks to friends and family who read *Plaguewalker* when it was young and still a bit wobbly: Tina Fitzgerald, Roberta Ganiere, and my brother, Matt Tarlach.

To my amazing editor and friend Dulcie Shoener, thank you for keeping my sins of grammar and punctuation our little secret. Thanks are in order also to fellow writers Doug Armstrong and Paul McComas, who offered both advice and enthusiasm as I prepared to send *Plaguewalker* out into the world.

And, most of all, to my mom, Audrey Duess: Thank you for indulging a little girl who liked to sit in her room alone and write about death.

The plague takes those who are afraid.

German proverb

1

I was born of the Devil. That is what they said. I was a conjure of night and fog, and the grave was the womb from which I emerged.

That is what they said.

It was November, when the first snows fell wet and heavy on brown brittle grass and trees stung leafless from the cold. Even the hardy conifers, rising up from the valley in thick fingers, where glen became hillside and then at last mountain, seemed to fade to a dull gray-green in the cold, their branches yawning under the snow's weight.

They found me in a basket, beside the cemetery gate. Their ragged funeral procession drew into a knot of whispering around me. The dead man they had come to bury was forgotten for a moment as they stared down at me.

A torn piece of cloak was all that shielded my naked, wailing body from frost-laced wind. My cries would not cease, they said. I punched the air with angry, walnut-sized fists as if to strike out at them all.

None of them would have me. All of them had mouths enough to feed already, and harvest that year had been poor.

No one stepped forward to claim a child of the Devil for his own.

In that cold dawn, the priest and the townspeople clustered around the basket, frowning down at the creature within it and wondering how they might be rid of me in such a way that would not stain their conscience. None of them wanted me.

So he took me.

He said the priest sent for him, but gave no message. He came out of curiosity, for no man of God had ever dared summon him. I can imagine the sight of him, trudging through drifts of snow, steam puffing out in white bursts from under his hood as he took shape from a cold mist.

All around him was white: snow, fog, frost-covered stones of the cemetery and the faces of those who awaited him. And yet he was black. No flesh was visible. Black boots to the knee, black trousers stained with old blood, black longshirt, and a lambskin vest taken from that unlucky animal born the Devil's color. A heavy woolen black cloak fell six feet from his broad shoulders, ending just above the snow. His black capuchon was drawn up against the cold. His leather hood of office fell down over his face, stiffened from beneath with thin metal boning to form a hideous mask: long, pointed nose, thick and frowning lips, a severe brow brooding over the eyeslits.

No wonder they thought him the man to decide the fate of the Devil's child.

"What is it?"

He was a man of few words, fewer even than I, and of short patience. They drew back from his growl, and the weaker ones shielded their eyes from him.

The priest cleared his throat, dry in the bitter wind. He pointed. "Someone has left a child here, a boy."

"What concern is it to me?"

There was a pause, for no one wanted to speak first and risk his stare. Then they opened their mouths as one, Babel rising anew in the frost and fog of the valley.

"Born on All Souls' from the look of him. The Day of the Dead!"

"His hair, the color of hell-flame!"

He rested his hands on his hips, and in doing so drew back his cloak that all might see his sheathed broadsword, pommel carved with his mark of office. The hush fell again.

His voice sliced through the air like a scythe. "Do you want me to kill it?"

The priest spoke again, nervous now. Perhaps he had been wrong to call for the man. "No, Meister Scharfrichter. I thought...the boy has no home. You have no son. Perhaps he has been left here for you."

He left the rest unsaid. There was no need to speak what was obvious, that my appearance augured badly and that no one would risk bringing ill luck across their thresholds, not even the priest.

The man behind the mask considered this. Then with the suddenness of a bull charging, he stormed toward them. They scattered, terrified.

He looked down at me, saw that I was well-formed and my color good, despite the cold. My shrieks alone were proof of healthy lungs.

Then he picked up the basket and tucked it under his arm as if it were a loaf of bread.

He turned his back on the cemetery and the silent crowd. And he carried me away from the town, skirting its fringes along the path to which he was restricted. I can see him, tree-trunk legs never breaking stride as he carried me up into the pine-covered hills, away from those who would not have me.

I remember none of this, of course. I only repeat the story I was told when I asked him once how I came to be the executioner's son.

2

"Let it be known by all that in this Year of Our Lord thirteen hundred and forty-nine, Hilde Schmidt of Ansberg has confessed to the murder of her newly born child, and that she is sentenced in accordance with the code of justice established by the Holy Roman Emperor."

The woman's head falls forward, smothering a sob that had threatened to disrupt the cold stateliness of Meister Schoeffen's chambers.

The chaplains help her into a cloak of fresh linen as colorless as the light snow that has begun to fall outside. None but babes carried to the baptismal font, and the condemned, wear white.

Her face is white as well, drained in terror and exhaustion. She is all bone, what little there is of her. One wonders how her body carried a hale child to term without flesh enough to support the mother, let alone the bastard boy. Between the chaplains she looks but a girl.

"Scharfrichter."

I nod to the Schoeffen and step forward to lead them from the room. Behind me, she sobs again. One of the chaplains murmurs admonishment.

The cloak of the condemned is too long for her small frame. I can hear it rustling behind me all the way from the room, down the stairs, out of the Rathaus, and into a cold Friday morning.

Outside, the clamor of those gathered drowns all other sound. The crowd presses against the Rathaus gate and fills the Marktplatz beyond it. Their winter-whitened faces leer at us, chapped lips curling under and shouting at the woman behind me.

"Loewe."

I say it quietly enough, but the sound of my voice is enough to silence the crowd. Jorg takes advantage of their sudden stillness and steps in front of me. His staff swings in an arc before us like a thresher's scythe.

They draw back as one shambling giant, leaving the gateway clear. As one they hold their breath and wait. Our silent procession passes under the gate and into the Marktplatz.

The crowd parts reluctantly to let us pass. Its cold-gruffed voice reawakens.

"Whore!"

"Killer of innocents!"

"To the Rabenstein! Justice be done!"

Jorg leads us around the edge of the square, swinging his staff in measured half-circles to clear the way. The woman and chaplains are behind me, the Schoeffen and his officers in the rear. Behind them the crowd closes in again.

A droplet of sweat breaks on my forehead. It tickles its way down my nose, into my mustache, then finally, teasingly, comes to a rest on my lip. It is always hot under the mask. My toes curl together from the cold, but my face is on fire. I would like nothing better than to throw off the metal and leather hood, breathe in air free of the stink of old sweat, and mop the glaze off my face.

It is of course forbidden. The Scharfrichter's face is not to be seen in public. I bite the sweat off my lips and frown.

It will be over soon enough.

A procession of the condemned cannot cross the age-worn cobblestones of the Marktplatz directly. Such an act would contaminate the town's commerce. So we circle around the perimeter of the square, under the shadows of its gabled shops and guildhalls.

Icicles from the long winter line their eaves like the teeth of a beast. Below the white and blue gleaming fangs, merchants and their families lean out of open windows that have been unshuttered so that all may watch the show. They leer and shout down at us, then wave to friends they recognize in the crowd squirming around our procession.

We turn down an alley that leads to the rear gate of the town, and the Rabenstein beyond it. Here the way is narrower, and the crowd presses in closer from all sides. Their jeers grate the ear like the cries of the ravens waiting for us past the city walls.

They are too close, and too many in number for the alleyway. We come to a standstill when onlookers ahead are blocked in by others pushing them back to catch a glimpse of the condemned.

"Back!" Jorg wields his staff clumsily in the confined space, trying to force an opening. The back end of the pole nearly clips me in the shoulder.

"Loewe! I lead!"

He glances back at me, alarm in his eyes. Then he steps to one side.

As I move into his place, the crowd quiets again. Men and boys who had but moments earlier laughed at Jorg now fall back. One drunk fool, in such a rush to avoid me, slips on the snow-slick cobbles and tumbles backward, taking three others with him.

I advance, needing no staff to clear the way.

I will deal with Jorg later, tomorrow even. He is not all at fault. He is small for a Loewe, and young. Like dogs sensing fear, the crowd could smell his hesitation and mocked him for it.

But they fear me.

To them I am still the flame-haired boy born on the Day of the Dead, now grown into a monster. I tower over them, bigger even than the man who raised me. I glare down at them all as I advance, the tallest man barely to my shoulder. They shudder and bow their heads.

They are cowards, hurling insults and clumps of frozen refuse at the woman behind me, but falling over themselves to avoid even brushing the edges of my black cloak.

We make our way steadily now, but without haste. The Schoeffen does not like us to hurry, though I would just as soon throw the woman over my shoulder and stretch my legs to their longest, the faster to be done with the day's work. But such haste would deprive the townspeople of their chance to see what befalls those who break the laws. Or so Meister Schoeffen says.

I think the crowd learns little of respect for the law from our measured steps. Likely they line the alleyways to give their throats a stretch, to shout words that would be deemed profane in another circumstance.

We pass under the dark stones of the Rabentor, under its graven images of a skull flanked by two ravens, and then out of town. Unmarked graves of suicides and killers stretch out to either side of us in trenches along the town walls. Jorg and I dug a fresh pit this morning, hard work in nearly frozen soil. The hole yawns black and ugly in the new snow as we pass it.

Behind me, the woman begins to sob again.

The Rabenstein is but fifty paces from us now. It is nothing but a platform of wood raised on mortared stones. Off the near side is a beam projecting from a post only inches taller than I, its wood splattered with old, burned pitch. As I mount the platform I notice that age has cracked the post near its base.

Jorg and I should fix that before spring.

The crowd assembles around the Rabenstein like hounds hoping for a morsel to be tossed their way. I hear the woman stumble on the platform stairs behind me. Likely the overlong hem of her cloak has tripped her.

I look back at her and frown again. She has the pallor of a near-faint about her. Her lips are almost blue in the cold.

Jorg's eyes are hard on me. I glance his way and nod, then turn my back. I do not need to watch to know that he is offering her a draught from a silver cask he carries at his belt. It is the duty of the Loewe to make the condemned drink. I had done it time enough when the man who raised me was Scharfrichter.

Thought of the last time I administered the strengthening draught deepens my frown.

I do not like this at all.

The crowd cheers, so I know that the woman has drunk. I turn halfway back to her and catch Jorg's eye again. He nods slightly, meaningful only to me. We both know what I am thinking.

I approach the woman. Her eyes roll back in her head and she nearly swoons. The chaplains steady her at the last instant. Jorg stares at me still, apprehension naked on his face.

"I ask your forgiveness."

I am required by law to say the words, just as the condemned are required to drink the dark, oily liquid the Loewe foists upon them. Whether any of them actually forgive me, I neither know nor care.

"Behold, Justice."

This I say louder, to the delight of the crowd. It convulses in an expectant cheer as I unsheathe my sword. A feeble ray of winter light glints off the word *Justica* engraved along the blade. It is longer than the sword of the man who raised me, and wider nearer the pommel, made to my design. I had commissioned a sword of my own upon becoming Scharfrichter. The last sword of that office was unlucky.

The chaplains do not linger. One of them is halfway down the platform steps before the crowd presses in and blocks further retreat. I wonder if the clerics are so eager to leave because they remember the risks of a beheading.

Jorg is as white-faced as the woman as he guides her to the middle of the platform. I look for a sign that the drink has taken effect: a stiffening of the spine, a raise of the chin. I watch for anything that will let me know she is ready. But she only trembles, head slumped near to her chest, her breathing ragged.

The crowd shifts, growing restless. Someone flings a handful of snow at us. It *thwaps* harmlessly onto my boots, but the sound of its impact makes the woman jump and shiver anew.

I do not like this at all.

Her whole girlish body convulses, whether from terror or cold I am not certain. But I am no longer cold. I am sweating now, as overheated as I was on a stifling summer noon when the man who raised me mounted the platform for what was to be his last time.

I had given the drink to the condemned, a narrow little man not much taller than a boy. And I had stood and watched as the Scharfrichter raised his sword.

Only I among those assembled knew that he had been drinking that morning, more even than on a usual morning. Only I saw the waver in his blade as he brought it down on the back of the condemned man's neck.

It was a clumsy swing, and at an awkward angle. The blade struck the man on the top of his head and cleanly sliced off his scalp. A circle of white skull gleamed in the June sunshine. The condemned man shrieked in pain and confusion. He lurched forward.

The Scharfrichter swung again, from the opposite angle, with even greater misjudgment. The blade hit home along the man's brow and stuck fast in bone and brain.

The crowd was in an uproar. They jeered and threw mud in wet, sloppy handfuls at the platform. I grabbed the bleeding mess of man, still alive and flailing, and tried to stand him up.

The Scharfrichter panicked. I jumped back as the blade sliced the air inches from my own neck. He was striking blindly now, in a drunken terror. He slashed air and man alike.

None of the blows was strong enough or certain enough to finish the job.

Some of the crowd overran a weak railing set up along the Rabenstein. They piled onto the platform, all of them enraged at the clumsy show.

I shoved the Scharfrichter aside, grabbing his sword as he stumbled back. And standing over the condemned wretch as he jerked and twitched in a pool of his own gore, I raised the blade once more. I brought it down hard on the narrow place at the back of his neck.

His head rolled forward, cleared of his shoulders, and was immediately lost in the flood of townspeople clambering all around me. But it was not me they wanted.

They grabbed the Scharfrichter by his cloak and hauled him off the platform, no longer afraid to be contaminated by his touch.

He had failed in his duty. He would pay.

I jumped into the mob, grabbing them in pairs. Big though I was, I was but one man. When they jumped me from behind I slipped in the mud and was trampled.

After the smother of angry, stomping bodies cleared, two pairs of sure hands helped me to my feet. It was the last time any of the town guards would touch me.

I lumbered to my feet like a bear and stared at the man who raised me.

It had taken the entire town garrison to break up the mob. I doubt even then that they would have succeeded, had the crowd not already achieved its goal.

The Scharfrichter's body, unmasked, naked, face down in the mud, was twenty paces from me. A man ignorant of the circumstances might have thought wild animals responsible for the killing.

Another snowball smacks against the Rabenstein.

I force myself to feel the sting of cold February air. Now is not the time to remember. I am the Scharfrichter now, and I have a job to do.

Jorg steadies the woman. His light eyes are large and wet with fear as he watches me. He was barely twelve years old on that summer day when the man who raised me, his father, was torn apart by the crowd as if by wolves. He remembers it as well as I.

I take a practice swing behind the woman. The crowd claps and yelps in excitement like the animals they are.

Another half-swing. The woman is too short. It is hard enough to strike the right place on a man of good size. But she is barely taller than my waist.

I grimace. Awkward as it is, I half-squat behind her, one leg extended to the side to brace myself.

Then I swing. The blade sings through the air, slicing into flesh and bone.

The force of the blow at so odd an angle staggers me. I spin around on one heel, searching for my balance.

The crowd shudders as one. Their eyes widen.

They begin to applaud.

The woman's head tumbles off to one side of the Rabenstein, one of her severed braids flying into the crowd to be seized as a souvenir.

3

Jorg glances up at me as he pats the black earth once more with the back of his shovel. He has been tracing idle patterns in the dirt for the last several minutes, waiting to catch my eye as I labor to finish our task.

"I heard one of the merchants talking. They say the dying has reached as far as Nuremberg."

I shrug and throw a last shovelful of dirt onto the grave. It is late already. We need to hurry to be home by nightfall. At least the snow has stopped.

"They say it traveled from the South on the back of its servant, the giant in black."

He presses his lips together, reconsidering his words as he stares up at me. But he is not one to be silent for long.

"Do you think it will reach us?"

I do not answer, but turn my back and start walking.

Jorg is too much like his mother. I hear him hurrying behind me, scampering like an eager puppy. He is nearly twenty, but there is something in his face that tells me he is not yet a man. There is an open look in his eyes, and a sloppy, too ready smile. I worry he will always be a boy.

"The merchant said it sleeps during winter, like the bears."

I ignore him. I have no desire to encourage his chatter, but neither is there much value in punishing him. I tried that once. He'd wept like a toddler.

We climb into the hills that roll up from the Rabenstein, following a steep trail only hinted at beneath the snow. It leads us into the pine forest where I played as a boy, alone except for a pair of the Scharfrichter's dogs that took a liking to me. Sometimes I would see a group of town boys racing and fighting and chasing each other in the meadow below, near the Rabenstein. I approached them only once. As they saw me descending along the Scharfrichter trail, they broke and ran like deer before a wolf. Their mothers and fathers had warned them that nothing good comes down that trail.

"Marcus, do you not hear me call for you to slow down?"

I glance over my shoulder at Jorg. I am so used to walking these hills alone that I forget how much longer my legs are than his. His face is red, streaming with sweat under his black capuchon.

"Hurry or I will leave you out here alone."

I walk faster now, forcing him into a run. The effort reduces him to silence.

A shadow in the trees ahead takes shape. The dog bounds toward us, kicking up small avalanches on the snow-covered slope. He is the size of a wolf, and with teeth to match. He hurdles over a fallen tree and throws himself against my chest.

I scratch the black ruff behind his ears. A good dog is worth ten men, even ten good men, a number I have yet to meet.

"Hund, Hund," Jorg singsongs behind me and is ignored. Hund is my dog. He nudges my hand for another scratch and then falls into a lope beside me.

Already I can see the lights of our house flickering yellow through gaps in the trees. The Scharfrichter has always lived outside of the town walls, as has his family. All of us who are shunned live out here in the hills. The night-soil workers, two families of them, live on the next ridge. There was a trio of lepers living in an old barn in the meadow higher up, behind our house, but I have not seen them in years and think they have died or moved on.

The whores, of course, live with us. There are only three left, and one of them is a crone who attracts no customers. When the man who raised me ran the brothel, there were a half dozen or so of them, and he saw to it they earned their keep. I have not his discipline, I suppose.

I smell onions in the cold evening air and walk faster. Jorg whines for me to slow down from somewhere in the nightgloom behind me. But I am already up the short set of stairs and through the door of my house, Hund at my heel.

The mask comes off first. Sweat flicks in all directions. I throw the mask along with my black gauntlets and cloak on a row of pegs near the door. The sword I leave in its scabbard, leaning against the near wall.

"Marcus, we've nearly starved waiting for you!"

I mop my brow. Tante smiles as she stands up from a low chair pulled beside the hearth, where she was tending a kettle. She offers me a clean cloth and bowl of water. The cool, damp linen feels good on my skin.

"Where is Jorg?" She glances behind me, as if thinking my foster brother is hidden behind my bulk. It is possible.

But at that moment he comes through the door after me, breathless and bright-faced.

The other women appear, like mice at the cupboard, from all corners: Gerta, old enough to have borne me, and the working whores Elise and Claudia. And last enters Sabine, Elise's daughter.

I sit down on the hard bench near the door to tug off my boots. My toes, numbed from the cold, reawaken in hot spasms of pain.

Sabine comes to me and sits at my feet beside Hund, to help me with my boots. She looks up at me from under thick lashes like the fringe of a woman's funeral shawl. Her green-gray eyes watch me with a teasing seduction she learned from her mother. She is but thirteen years old, and as fine as Elise, who still lures men up to the house even in the deepest of winter.

But Sabine is not a whore. And I am not a man she can practice her wiles upon.

"Leave me. Go help Tante."

She frowns, lips curling under in a pout that likely she has practiced for hours in front of her mother's polished metal mirror.

"Someone left this at the door." Elise steps between us, skirts rustling in Sabine's face. "I saw only his back. He would not stop to give his name."

I take the folded parchment gingerly. It is of fair quality, the sort of paper used for court records, and sealed with a purple blob of wax. I tuck it into my shirt. I will read it later, when I am alone.

"What is it? Tell us!" whines Sabine, tugging on my belt as I stand. She is tall for her age, and not at all frail. Even as I brush her aside, I notice that she is growing into a woman before me, and a beautiful one at that. More beautiful than her mother, I think.

"Now we eat."

I do not mind conversation at meals, unlike the man who raised me, as long as I am not expected to participate. Let Jorg and the women chatter, I do not care. I usually do not notice. The many hours I have spent at work in the Falterkammer have inured me to distraction.

But tonight is different. Jorg cannot stop talking about the dying.

"Merchants waiting to pay taxes at the Rathaus told me they saw it strike last month as they traveled to market in Nuremberg. They said all of them were inspected by guards before they were allowed to sell in the Marktplatz. The guards looked in their armpits, where it sometimes hides. They say it turns into a black egg with the face of the Devil himself."

"It has struck in Nuremberg, then?" Tante clucks her tongue.

Elise snorts under her breath. "It would be good for it to come here and clean out the town."

"Meister Scharfrichter, have you ever seen the dying?" Sabine asks.

I glance at her suddenly earnest eyes, her hand hovering above mine as if to show regard without distracting me from my bowl of stew. She is being so polite because she wants to know what is in that letter.

"No more talk of the dying." Then I look over at her mother. Elise, with her pink skin and white-gold hair, is still a beauty. But she pales beside her daughter, with a face like moonlight upon snow. Sabine has eclipsed her and she knows it. I wonder if she is jealous yet.

"And you will not wish it here, Elise."

They frown at me as one, both denied.

I eat the last of the bread. The women clean the table, looking at me sidelong, wondering about the letter. Only Jorg shows no interest. Likely he is sore from grave-digging. I watch his back disappear down the hall that leads to a narrow ladder, up to their bedrooms, and I wonder. I wonder how he could be the son of the man who raised me, and yet but a slip of a boy, and a simple one at that.

"Are you going to read the letter?" Gerta asks with a croak, voicing the question all of them want answered.

Without replying, I turn my back and feed the last crust of bread to Hund. I leave the women and pretend to sort through a large wooden coffer I keep on a table beside the hearth.

I take a careful inventory, though I already know which powders and extracts I will need to replenish soon. It will be easy enough to draw more sap from the Sadebaum, which suffers little in winter. The tree is not so plentiful on our hillsides, but I know well enough where to find its dark berries and sharp-needled limbs.

Ah, but finding more of the pale, feathered Wermut leaves will be impossible this time of year. I should have collected more of the plant, before the snows and cold. It is not like me to forget.

Then I remember what happened the last time I went out with my basket under my arm, to search out the leaves and fronds and soft berries that I need. Sabine had decided to accompany me. Skipping back and forth before me, always in my way though I warned her off, she tumbled all at once as we climbed up an incline of scree.

Her ankle turned, not bad enough to break the bone, but such that I had to stop and bind the injury. Then I carried her back down the hill when she would not walk on her own but instead wailed loud enough to rouse all the forest birds.

By the time I handed her over to the women, it was too late in the day to search out the last of the year's Wermut. The snows began soon after.

I frown at my oversight and set the last of the stoppered jars and vials each in its accustomed place, inside the casket older than anyone still alive, and engraved with the initials of someone I do not know. Perhaps the father of the man who raised me. I never asked him about the carved letters, nor did he ever care to offer explanation on his own. I fasten the latch and wipe a fine layer of dust from the lid.

When at last I glance over my shoulder, only Elise remains.

"It is from Lindau, is it not?"

I glare at her. "Have I read it yet?"

"You will read it to me. It is my right."

There are times I wish I could strike out as easily as had the man who raised me. For him, punches were punctuation, expected in even the briefest of conversations. I do not know why I hold back. Perhaps, early on, he beat out any temper I had. Or perhaps because I know there is little gain in expending the effort to cross the room, to hit her and throw her to the floor, she who already endured years of it before I became Scharfrichter. And still she was stubborn.

She will have to wait. I am in no rush to read the letter, for I know that it cannot contain anything good.

"Read it now, in front of me."

I turn my back on her again. Elise has always had a streak of the Devil about her. When she first came to the brothel, the men complained she bit, she scratched, she taunted them. The man who raised me tried to beat submission into her, but failed. The house became their battlefield in a war of wills, his every punishment of her answered with another transgression.

The worst of it came when she grew round with Sabine. She would not drink the whore's brew that bleeds out the baby, so that the woman's ability to turn a profit can continue uninterrupted.

The man who raised me nearly killed her over that show of impudence. He would have, I think, had I not intervened. By then I was already bigger than he, and his will was ever more addled by drink.

I think of Elise as she was one night soon after Sabine was born. The moon spilled in from an open window over the bed and turned her pale hair silver where she lay. She rolled off of me and out from a thin summer blanket.

"Do you want me to marry you?"

She glanced back at the sound of my voice, her fair brow rippled. "Whatever for?"

"For Sabine. She is my daughter. Perhaps you should be my wife."

"Frau Scharfrichter?" She rolled her eyes. "I'd rather be dead."

"Or a whore?"

She stared out the window, into the night. "Better to be a whore, able to go to market and to walk where I please."

I never asked again. I did not love Elise, but her words were cold on my skin even in the warm summer air of thirteen years ago. Even a whore would prefer her way of life to mine.

My fingers brush the wax seal of the letter in my pocket absently.

Elise is gone. She must have given up on me, lost in my reminiscing. Yes, I was right to be silent. She cannot stand silence. It drives her away.

I sit, drawing my bench nearer to the low fire sputtering in the hearth. The letter, out of my pocket and in my callused hand, looks smaller than when Elise held it. Smaller and perhaps less significant.

I recognized the seal at once. Meister Scharfrichter von Lindau. I met him years ago when he came to visit the man who raised me. They were friends of sorts, trained under the same Scharfrichter when they were less than Jorg's age. I remember him as a bullish man, bald with a thick neck that spread out into massive sloped shoulders. He had a son in Lindau, a few years my senior.

I slit the wax open with my thumbnail. The seal cracks, half of it falling to the floor.

The message inside is brief. All of us who work in the Falterkammer can read and write, of course. We must have both skills, to keep records of the torture administered, the confessions made. But none of us are trained to be florid in our language.

"Meister Marcus von Ansberg: Your letter received. My one grandson is already married. Our family has no other sons to marry your daughter. Meister Karl von Lindau."

I expected as much. I thought too late of the proposal. Already I had asked the Scharfrichters at Erfurt and Nuremberg. Now I will have to look further yet.

"What does it say?"

Elise was more clever than I thought. She must have hid in the shadows of the ladder, listening for the sound of parchment being opened. I read the message aloud.

"Good. I forbid her from marrying a Scharfrichter."

"You would sooner I turn her out to whore?"

"She is my daughter. I will decide what to do with her."

But she backs against the wall under my glare. Stupid woman. She knows as well as I that Sabine can never marry a townsman, even one from another town. No one wants the daughter of a whore and an executioner, and with no dowry to speak of. Only another Scharfrichter, out of pity or his own desperation, might offer a son in marriage.

Elise cannot stand the silence between us for long.

"You were wrong to write to him, to all of them, begging them to take Sabine from me! Your own blood, and you would condemn her to a life of death!"

Her shouts will wake the others. I shake her hard by the shoulders, but it only fuels her anger.

"You bastard! You would sell her, no, give her away to strangers!"

She throws up her hands too late. My hand catches her across the jaw. She staggers backward.

The sob comes from behind me. Sabine stands there in the shadows, her hair, the same devilish shade as her father's, falling in a tumble over her nightdress. She stares at me through a mist of tears.

"Go back to bed. Now."

"You? My father?"

Her face contorts as if she is in pain.

Elise never told her the truth. She filled her head with fanciful tales of a knight who died gloriously in some battle far from our dull little town.

I never thought to tell Sabine otherwise. I have no desire to speak to her of it now.

"Go on, girl. Now."

She runs. Whether from sight of her mother in a heap at my feet or from the truth of her father, I do not know.

4

Tap-tap-tap.

The tentative knock at my door comes in the thick of the witching hour. I hold my breath, listening for it again.

"Meister Scharfrichter?" It is a broken whisper, the sound of a young woman cried hollow.

I roll away from the door and wait for her to give up. I have nothing to say to Sabine.

"Someone has come for you."

I open my eyes and throw off the bedclothes. Cold air stings my flesh all over. Even in winter I sleep naked, beneath an old quilt that smells of Hund. It is the only way I can sleep, free of the mask and workclothes that reek of blood. I find my shirt and trousers and tug them on. My feet I leave bare, though my toes curl under from the cold.

I open the door suddenly, surprising her. She stares down at the floor.

"A woman has come, and says she must speak with you alone."

I can guess what it is about. Sabine does not step aside. I cannot leave my room without pushing her. She looks up then, blue shadows from tears and worry ringing her pale eyes.

"Why did you never tell me, about being my father?"

"Stand aside, girl."

She does not so much move as crumple, turning away from me and falling against the doorjamb, sobbing anew. I wonder if all women are so easily given to tears, or if the weakness is peculiar to Elise's blood. I have never seen Tante or the others cry so freely.

The front door is open, moonlight outlining a short, round shape that shrinks back from the threshold when she hears me. Sabine has not lit either of the lamps in the room, so my visitor cannot see me clearly. That is good, for I do not have my mask of office on yet. I find it on one of the pegs near the door and throw it on.

"What is it?"

I scrape a flint along the flagstone nearest the threshold, and set the spark to one of the lanterns I keep beside the door for occasions such as this. Crouching on the floor, I see only her skirts, colored dim orange by the fledgling light. As I rise, drawing up the lantern with me, I see she is fat, and young, three summers older than Sabine perhaps. Her skirts lead up to a thick waist. Edges of long gold braids peep out beneath a shawl drawn close in the cold. She has no cloak. She must be freezing. I glance at her feet and see that her worn boots are crusted with snow.

Her face is broad, dominated by large gray eyes. Sweat breaks out along her white brow despite the cold.

She stares up at me, towering over her like the demon she probably thinks me to be. I wonder if she notices my hands are white and pinched from the cold night air that crosses over the threshold, even if she will not.

"Meister...Meister Schfu…" The effort uses up the last of her confidence.

I do not wait for another attempt at address. I am used to stuttered greetings. "Come inside. It is cold."

She nods too quickly, as if relieved that I can sense the chill as humanly as she. "Th-th-thank you, Meister Schaf…Meister Scharf…"

"What is it, then?"

I move around the room easily in the darkness. Its spare furnishings have not been rearranged since before I was born. At last I light the hearth, for her benefit. She stays near the door.

"Tell me, girl, why you have come."

I know already. The night visitors are not so rare. Sometimes it is an old man or woman, or the relative of one struck by illness. Sometimes it is a young mother whose child has been seized with fever. They come seeking help, the kind of help only the Scharfrichter can give. They ask for blood from the beheaded, the ear from a thief, the hand of a murderer, something they think will cure them, protect them, give them another year to live.

But the young maids come for only one thing.

She does not answer, fear sticking in her throat.

"How far along are you?" I ask at last. I would like to sleep some before dawn yet. There is no need to prolong this.

She sucks in a tight little breath. I wonder which farmhand or merchant's son it was who lured her behind a barn or into a dark alley. Maybe I am wrong. Maybe she did the seducing.

"Three months."

That is bad. It is best to drink the brew early, before the child settles in the womb. That is what the man who raised me taught me, anyway. He showed me the proper dosage for that drink and a dozen others to cool fevers or stave off infection. So too he showed me how to dry the ears and hands of the executed so that eager buyers could hand over their money for the relics.

Of course, he took not only money from them. Pleasure, too. He would tell the young maids, terrified to be with child, that only his seed could kill their unwanted offspring. He'd mount them there in front of the hearth, desperate creatures whose piteous cries echoed through the whole house. Jorg and I would wake, and sometimes creep to the edge of the doorway to watch with a mix of fear and fascination. The whores slept through it. A woman's cries never woke them.

I turn my back on her and select a few vials from the coffer beside the hearth. It is not so complicated a recipe, little more than a mix of pale Wermut leaf powder and a good bit of the crushed heart-shaped leaves of Hirtentaschel, all poured into a goblet. I drown it in wine and swish it around to mix. A drop slops out onto my hand. It looks like blood.

"How much can you pay?"

She makes that sucking noise once more. She has a basket with her, I remember. Ah, it seems I will get paid in chickens again.

She offers it to me. Under a thin cloth are more than a dozen eggs, more than I could eat at three sittings, even if I liked eggs. I do not.

"Underneath the eggs."

Taking them out carefully—if nothing else, Tante can pickle them—I see a shimmer of blue beneath. It is a few lengths of fabric, but nothing a farmer's daughter like her might possess. I do not know cloth, but even I can tell from its soft luster that it is silk.

"Where did you steal this from?"

"I didn't steal it!" She shrinks back from me. "It is from the boy. He cut it from a bolt in his father's shop as payment. His father has plenty. He'll not notice it missing."

Sometimes my mind wanders. Too often, I think. For a moment, staring down at the sapphire fabric, I think of Sabine. This is a rich woman's cloth, and it would make her a fine dress. A dress fine enough to pretend she is something other than the daughter of a Scharfrichter.

"Please, I have nothing else." The girl begins to sputter, fresh tears running down either side of her bulbous nose.

I nod. I hand her the goblet and she drinks sloppily. Even before she finishes, I tell her the herbs may not work. She came to me late.

"You should be sick for a few days, and then bleed it out."

Her whole face quivers when she tries to set it in a courageous expression. Then she is gone, backing out through the door, leaving her basket behind. I put the eggs inside it and leave it on the table for Tante to find in the morning. The silk I roll up under my arm and take back to my room. I leave it on an old trunk and slide back under the covers.

I am awake before any of them. Usually Tante is up first, heating water in a kettle over the hearth, portioning out the smallest bit of spelt that she can use for bread, chasing mice back into their holes. But today I wake up long before dawn. Sometimes it is that way, when I know I will be spending long hours in the Falterkammer.

I am surprised to see I left the front door open. I thought I had closed it. The air in the room is so cold that frost is collecting on a stack of kindling near the dark hearth.

Outside it is only a little colder. I squat in the snow and scoop handfuls of it into a bowl. Relighting the hearth, I let the snow warm slowly, until it is water. Then I shave.

I do not keep a full beard. It would suffocate me beneath the mask, working beside a hot fire in the small Falterkammer. For a while I kept myself clean-shaven. But the metal boning of my mask chafed against my chin. So I grew a wedge of beard just around and under my mouth.

Jorg tries to copy me, scraping off the silky white hairs that collect in tufts along his jaw. He does not handle a sharp blade as well as I, however, and his skin is marked with nicks and scars.

Commotion breaks out above me. Upstairs, where the whores sleep, something has happened. I hear shouts and wailing. It sounds like Elise.

"You bastard!" She flies down the stairs, giving me but a moment to draw the blade away from my throat before she plows into me. The knife and bowl of melted snow clatter to the floor.

"You drove her away! Your own blood!"

I throw her off. Tante and the other women join us, their faces pale and anxious in the gray light of dawn.

Elise rolls to her feet, and would strike me again if I let her. I shove her backward. She hits the wall and collapses to the floor, too hysterical now to make sense as she screams at me.

"Sabine is missing," Tante says lowly. She kneels down to Elise and glances up at me. I am surprised to see accusation in her eyes.

"Pissing behind the woodshed, probably." I glare at Elise for churning all of them up for nothing.

"No. Her good dress and boots are gone. She took everything." Claudia says this, the same Claudia we figured a mute for years after her father sold her to the man who raised me. I do not think I have heard so many words from her in all the years I have known her.

It was Sabine, then, who left the door open.

Jorg wobbles down the steep ladder stairs, rubbing his eyes and looking to me for explanation. They are all looking at me.

"You should go look for her, Marcus." Tante has never chided me before.

I frown at her, then turn to clean up the mess Elise made of my toilet.

"Go find her, bring her back to me, or you are not a man!" shrieks Elise, suddenly lucid again. She has gone too far.

"You forget who you are talking to, whore," I say sharply, wiping the blade dry on the edge of my trousers.

Elise stands, her face blood-red. "No, I know I am talking to the coward who would run his own blood out of the house, and not be man enough to bring her back!"

The lob of spittle hits me in the face.

I barrel through them to her, and grab her by the hair. Shrieks and cries break out all around me, the way sheep raise a chorus when the wolf lays hold to one of them.

I pull her outside, down the stairs on her knees, and throw her headfirst into a snowbank. She is lucky I am not given to anger, for I could do far worse.

"You go find her, whore. I have work to do."

Shivering in her thin gown, the snow clumping in her hair, she falls silent. She shakes, and claws handfuls of snow. To throw at me at any moment, I suspect.

Then I glance past her, down the hill and past the snug walls of the town, beyond the twin spires of the church and the dark stone of the Rathaus, out toward the west horizon where day is still sleeping. Movement catches my eye.

On the white ripples of hills, farmland slumbering until the thaw, I see a serpent. It is a long, narrow, black snake, slithering its way along the Nuremberg road toward our town. I cannot see it clearly at this distance, but know it is a long parade of people, moving as one dark animal. I can guess what it is.

"Jorg, fetch my mask and gloves."

I do not wait for him. He can run to catch up with me. I leave Elise quivering in the snow and start down the trail toward town.

5

The serpent of people passes in and out of my sight through the trees as I hurry along the trail. I can see their banner carriers well enough to know they are Geissler, Brethren of the Cross.

I have overheard guards in the Rathaus speak of these men, who believe they can repent only by whipping themselves. I have also heard that their wild rituals provoke their audiences to mischief. Usually they incite townspeople to burn down the Jews' homes, but sometimes even that is not enough and they wreck the Marktplatz or cause some other unrest.

I do not rush to town to join them, or even to gawk as they perform whatever rite they believe assures them Paradise. I walk fast, as fast as my long legs can carry me, because the Scharfrichter is restricted to certain routes in the city. If the flagellants and their spectators block my way to the Rathaus, I will not be able to do the day's work in the Falterkammer. And I must, for I have unfinished business there.

Jorg catches up with me, panting, carrying my mask and gloves. I put them on, glad for once for the leather covering my face. It is a cold morning.

"Marcus, will you not look for Sabine?"

I start walking again.

"If you will not, then let me!"

I roll my eyes under the hood. The boy could not find a raven on a snowfield, much less a pouting little girl run off in the night. But I have no executions scheduled for the day, and do not need the services of the Loewe. In fact, for what I must do today, it is better not to have Jorg around. He has a weak stomach.

"Go then."

His feet make a crunching noise through the snow as they fade up the hill behind me. But my attention is on the Brethren. Already they are passing under the Haupttor and into town. I walk faster.

"HEE-YAH!"

The horse nearly tramples me.

The white stallion seems to emerge from the snow itself. I stagger as the boy and his mount thunder past. He is Sabine's age, and snickers at me over his shoulder as he crosses the path and disappears back into the forest.

I know the horse, and the dark-eyed boy on it. It is one of the Ritter's sons, snot-nosed brats all of them. I do not waste breath shouting after him.

Reins of another horse jingle behind me. Someone else is coming through the forest in the boy's wake. I turn just as he appears between two pines. The Ritter himself, on a fine roan, man and horse in red and maroon velvet, blood colors vivid against the white snow.

He sees me. No man could miss me, all in black and nearly the size of one of those pines, standing directly in front of him. He looks through me, though, as do all of the nobles. The poor have not been conditioned so, and stare or shrink back from sight of me. But he has mastered the skill of ignoring those beneath him. Perhaps the better breeds are born with it.

"Your boy's horse nearly trampled me."

Ritter Leonhardt allows his eyes to focus on me, staring down his long nose with a smirk. Though mounted on his horse, he is not much taller than I.

"Scharfrichter, you would speak to me?" He makes a snorting noise like that of his horse as it huffs out clouds of white air. "You were in his way, as you are now in mine."

I see now that they were hunting. His bow is slung over his shoulder, and a fat hare caught out of its warren dangles from his saddle. That hare should be mine, for my home is the nearest to these hunting grounds. But the Scharfrichter is forbidden from hunting anything, except wolves. As they make for poor eating, I never learned the bow.

I fold my arms over my chest. This man may hunt, ride a horse, and walk freely through the town, all things I cannot do by law. But I will not stand aside for him.

I stare at him for a long moment. And then he is afraid. Perhaps, behind all that arrogance, he remembers that while he holds titles, lands, and freedom, I hold the executioner's sword, and the keys to the Falterkammer.

He negotiates the horse around me, leaving a wide space. Then he is gone, back into the trees after his reckless son. I continue toward town.

Even as I pass under the mute stone ravens of the Rabentor, I hear a clamor rising from the Marktplatz. The human serpent has arrived already. I catch a glimpse of them, filing into the church on the opposite side of the square, as I head for the rear entrance of the Rathaus.

The back door is shorter than most, and even a man of modest height must dip his head under the lintel. I have to fold myself nearly in half. Inside there is nothing but a narrow set of stairs, leading down into darkness.

Meister Lockwirt has forgotten to light the way again. Drunk, probably. Or perhaps he has laid an ambush for me. He did so once, when I was still Loewe, dousing the torches and rigging a string across the stairs so I would be sure to misstep and tumble into his lair. Once I landed, he was on me like a bear on a fat fish. The man who raised me, following behind me and aware of the trap, lit a lantern and held it up to watch, laughing.

"I told you, Gilg, he is a big lad, but docile as a deer."

I heard the words in a muddle as I tried to scramble to my feet. The man rolled over me, his full weight landing on my skull and nearly crushing it. He paused to catch his breath and join in the laughter.

"That is because you never taught him to fight. Were he my boy, I would see he knew how to brawl."

He was distracted for a moment by his own guffaws. Enough that I was able to kick out from under him and flip over onto my knees.

"Agile though, like a cat, even as tall as he is."

The man who raised me grabbed a handful of my hair and yanked me to my feet. "There's only one cat needed here, and it's not you. Now to work, boy. Fetch the cat."

And without explanation for the whole incident he sent me farther down the corridor, to get a street cat we had locked in a small cage days earlier, starving it until it would be mad with hunger. The man who raised me needed it in the Falterkammer that morning.

I do not use cats, now that I am Scharfrichter. It seems too much trouble to starve a cat until it is ready to be placed on a prisoner's chest, and the bottom of its cage slid out, so that the animal, smelling flesh and a chance for escape, claws and bites its way into the gut. I prefer simpler means of extracting confessions.

Besides, I have no desire to skulk the alleys at night looking for cats, and I suspect Jorg would be hopeless at the task.

I feel my way down into the gloom of the jail, listening. I hear nothing. The Lockwirt is drunk then, rather than in a playful mood.

At the bottom of the stairs is a small chamber, with two corridors forking off in opposite directions. The whole of it stinks of dirt and human waste. I turn left, away from the hall that leads to the prisoners' cells and the small room where the Lockwirt has lived most of his life. I follow instead the corridor that leads to my workplace.

I smell him before I see him. So, he has decided to ambush me after all. I am but ten paces from the door of the Falterkammer when he strikes a flint against the stone wall and sets a torchiere ablaze.

He stares at me, piggish eyes slowly focusing. He is huge. I am a head taller than he, and not a narrow man, but I lack his sheer bulk. His bald head spreads out into jowls and rolls of flesh where other men have necks, then broadens into massive shoulders and a belly that presses against either side of the narrow corridor.

"You workin' the Jew today, yes?" He licks his lips, idly scratching his crotch. "Let me help."

I shake my head. But I cannot proceed. He fills the corridor in front of me. A waif like Jorg might squeeze past, but I am too big. I start to back out instead, to let him out first.

"You let me help. Bastard's been giving me his evil eye two days now."

Gilg likes to help in the Falterkammer, but I rarely allow it. He is a man who enjoys inflicting pain. The man who raised me was like that, outside the Falterkammer, too. He was more willing than I to accept Gilg's assistance.

Without Jorg this morning, though, I could use an extra pair of hands. At least in the beginning. Then maybe the drink will catch up with Gilg and he will stumble off to his cot.

"All right then. Go get him. But say nothing to him. Nothing."

He listens to me. He is old enough to be my father, but he respects what I do in the Falterkammer, especially when he is allowed to assist. He nearly bowls me over in his rush to fetch the prisoner.

At the end of the corridor, my corridor, is a single door. Its wood is stained black. Above the elaborate lock is a large knob, fashioned in the shape of a skull. The man who raised me paid plenty for it, believing it made the proper impression on visitors to the room beyond.

Inside the Falterkammer, it is a murky gray. There is one window, barely the size of my hand, set near the ceiling along the far wall. A heavy grate over it negates any benefit of light or fresh air. But that is not its purpose. It faces onto the Marktplatz, that my work might be heard by all and strengthen their resolve to obey the law.

The ceiling here is twice as high as elsewhere in the jail. Across its length is a wide brace, rigged with a pulley and a rope, ends of which dangle in the darkness. I brush past them on my way to light the hearth.

The small fire heats the room quick enough. Its light glints off my tools. I stoke the fire absently, leaning against the Fass. The old wooden cradle is large enough for a man and lined with spikes inside. I use it rarely. Like the cat, it is too elaborate for my taste. And too often, when I was Loewe and charged with tying the prisoner inside and then rocking the Fass back and forth as hard as I could, letting its spikes shred skin like the jaws of a wolf, I noticed that the motion dizzied and confused the prisoner.

It is too hard to get a confession when a man does not have his wits about himself.

I check over the table near the hearth, lined with tongs and torches, brands and pincers. My eyes linger on the Kranz. It may be useful to me today.

I can hear them approaching. Gilg throws the man into the Falterkammer and grins when the prisoner trips and falls in front of me. I wait for him to struggle to his feet, but he does not.

I crouch down, studying the back of his head as he lies face to the floor and motionless. A bruise has formed under his shorn hair, and a curve of dried blood crusts around one ear. This was not my work.

I glance at Gilg, reprimanding him silently. The wound is not uncommon for prisoners here. It is the Lockwirt's work. He grabs the man by the ear through the bars of his cell and bashes his head against the iron. Sometimes Gilg has done it hard enough, or time enough, that the man's head breaks open and he dies. And then he is of no use to me, for lacking a confession I cannot charge the town for my services. I do not think Gilg considers this when he does it, however. He is probably too busy laughing.

I twist the back of the man's shirt and haul him up by one hand, dragging him to a chair beside the hearth.

"You have rested these two days, since we last spoke?" In the Falterkammer, I choose my words with more care. The man who raised me taught me this. It is important the prisoner know he is dealing with a professional, not another brute like Gilg. "Perhaps you have something to say to me."

The man is my age, but thin and small. He is losing his black hair, though I do not think it is of any concern to him. He knows he will not live long enough to lose much more of it.

He looks up at me then, and rests his bony elbows on the chair's arms. I see defiance burning in his dark eyes. Ah, I knew it was going to be a long day.

"Well then, I will remind you why you are here. You have been accused of poisoning the well beside the Sudtor, resulting in the severe illness of Meister Kester and his family, and the death of his infant son. What say you?"

He draws in a breath as lightly as a sleeping maid. "I say, as before, I have not done this. I have never even been to the Sudtor well."

"I know the Jews have their own well, in their quarter of the city." I nod slightly, then turn partway and pick up the Kranz from the table. I have not used it on him yet, so perhaps he does not understand what it is. Now it looks merely like four straps of leather, studded in places and sewn together into something resembling a horse's bridle. I turn it over in my hands absently, and look up at him again. "But four witnesses saw you near the well the night before Kester fell ill."

"I tell you, I have never been in that quarter."

He is strong of will for such a narrow little man. I have already spent an afternoon with him. Yes, I will need the Kranz, but not yet. I must break him down a little first.

"Aufziehen."

Gilg jumps at the word like a dog who smells meat. He rushes over to the ropes dangling from the ceiling, a pair of iron cuffs attached to one end.

I pick up the man easily and throw him over one shoulder. He does not resist. On our first meeting, I put him in the Boot. His legs are still mangled from the vise. I don't think he could struggle much, even if he wanted to.

I stand him up, even let him lean against me a little as I put his wrists in the cuffs and tighten screws along their inner edge so that his scrawny hands don't slip through. He stares at the wall.

"How are your legs this morning?" My voice is low, well-suited to murmuring. In the small space of the Falterkammer it sounds like hell purring. I pause, though I know he will not answer. "Who was it who put the salve on them, and wrapped them in clean bandages for you? Who was it who offered you drink to ease the pain?"

His jaw clenches in response.

"It was I. I am not here to harm you, only to help you admit the truth. If you tell me the truth, I will let you go back to your cell and rest. I will even give you clean bandages."

Sometimes I am silent in the Falterkammer, nothing but a black shadow that moves around the prisoner as Death circles the ailing. But for men of some learning like him, I speak. It troubles them. They do not want me to be polite, to sound like one of their own.

His mouth trembles for a moment. Then his face closes again. He is not ready yet.

I gesture to Gilg, who is already grabbing the other rope. He leers. With a hard jerk, harder than I would have liked, he pulls on the rope, and the prisoner's arms rise over his head. Another pull, and his feet lift off the ground. I signal Gilg to stop when the prisoner is at my eye level.

"Have you anything to say?"

He shakes his head violently, like a dog shaking off water.

I crouch beside a large bucket near the table. It weighs nearly as much as Gilg, and I could never lift it. But I do not need to. Inside are several weighted chains, each with a cuff at one end. I select two of different weights.

Letting the weights rest on the ground, I put his ankles in the cuffs. Usually I choose two chains of the same poundage. Using different weights can force a man's hips out of their sockets if it is not done properly. But I am confident enough.

I signal again to Gilg. It is harder for him to pull the prisoner higher, now that he is dragging the weights. Gilg is easily strong enough for the task when he is sober, but this morning he falters when the man is halfway to the ceiling. I yank on the rope, helping him pull it the rest of the way.

"Have you anything to say?"

I see the glint of dread in the prisoner's eyes. We have done this before, he and I. He knows what is to come. But still he is silent.

I nod to Gilg. We let go of the rope together.

The man crashes to the floor in a heap, his way sped by the weights. I hear him choke back a cry.

"Have you anything to say?"

His voice is muffled, but I can make out the single word. No.

I gesture once more to Gilg, who hauls the man up toward the ceiling.

I do not like to drop a man more than twice. In the first fall, he is usually too tense, too fearful, and his body stiffens. Ankles sprain, bones break. In the second fall, stunned from the first, his body is looser and he is less likely to be hurt. But by the third time, he has recovered his fear, and tenses again, only now with splintered limbs. And that is bad. He could shatter an already fractured bone on impact, exposing the marrow. Then infection is more likely. I do not have time to deal with infections. Even if I did, here in Gilg's pit under the Rathaus, the squalid conditions would make treating them a lost cause. And if the man dies in prison, I do not get paid.

So I drop him only once more. This time he slumps to the ground as if lacking bones.

I pick him up again, noticing the wobble in his left leg. The knee has been damaged, shattered perhaps, for thin men such as he often have weak bones. I will have to bind it when we finish.

I set him in the chair. Gilg frowns at my shoulder. The Kranz is not dramatic enough for him.

Once the man is fastened to the chair with leather straps across his arms and chest, I pick up the Kranz and let him see it. He looks it over. Even through a daze of pain, I can see his mind working, wondering.

"Have you anything to say?"

He shakes his head, tongue lolling out of his mouth. He bit it during one of the drops. Blood oozes onto his lips.

I drape the Kranz over his head. It is important that the device be put on evenly. The leather straps crisscross over his forehead, metal studs at either temple and at the jaw joint. The metal cup on the chin strap is a little wide for his narrow face. But it will do.

I start to tighten the straps, twisting a leather lead running from the back of the device.

"Have you anything to say?"

He gasps as the metal studs press in at his temples and along his jaw, but is otherwise silent.

Now the straps are as tight as I dare. I slip a metal pin onto the lead, setting the tightness. Then I come around to his front, and lean so that my mask is inches from his face.

"Have-you-an-y-thing-to-say?" With each syllable, I tap on the chin cup. The taps are amplified by the Kranz, and reverberate through his head as if he were standing under a church bell.

"Nnnnggggguh!" His eyes tear from the effort.

I wait a moment. He shudders, and his eyes roll back in his head.

The straps loosen quickly under my gloved fingers. But he is already unconscious.

On my table is a small basket of vials. I choose one and open it under his nose. It stinks. But the smell is welcome in the small room, already reeking with sweat and pain and Gilg's vomit-tinged breath.

The prisoner's head jerks upward, eyes opening.

"Have you anything to say?"

He nods. I reach for a page of vellum, my quill, and a small bottle of ink. I let him see what I am doing, and hold the quill within his reach. I do not care if I write the confession and he signs it or if he does it all himself. As long as it gets recorded.

He makes no move for the quill. Instead he stares at me, eyes dry. He is past the point of pain, I worry.

"What say you?"

"I say..." His bloody tongue works back and forth, as if trying to assure him his jaw is still there, and not in pieces on the floor. "I say you will live forever."

I stare. I do not understand. His eyes are inches from mine, only my mask and a whisper of air between us.

Gilg shifts behind me, impatient for another round to begin. I wave him away.

"Leave us. Now."

I do not turn my eyes from my prisoner. Gilg shuffles off and slams the door behind him, but I do not hear it until later. Now I am too focused on the narrow man before me and his curious words. I shove the vellum and quill at him.

He nods slightly, showing he will write. I free one hand for him, and hold a wooden board against the back of the vellum so that he may record his confession. It is one sentence, with all the facts needed, and a signature. It will do.

I leave it on the table, so the ink can dry without smudging. He stares at me still.

Using a sharp dagger, I slice off what is left of his trousers. The legs are worse than I thought. One knee is already swelling, and an ankle turns at a bad angle.

I take my gloves off for this. It is important to do a careful job. Even with a confession, if the prisoner dies before sentence is passed, I earn nothing from it.

He does not respond as I pack the open wounds with a sweet-smelling poultice of dark Beinwell leaves. The breaks and sprains I can only wrap tightly, so tight that he will be numb to the pain. It does not matter if the blood flow is stopped by the pressure. He will be dead soon enough, hanged from the gallows beside the Rabenstein.

I feel his eyes on me. They burn with hatred.

"You will tell me, *Jude*, why I will live forever." I keep my voice flat. I am curious about his words, but do not want to show it.

He waits for me to meet his eyes. I see pain in them, and a desperation that could make a man admit anything, regardless of guilt or innocence. I know the look well.

"You will live forever because God does not want you, and the Devil is afraid you will overthrow him."

I stare back but say nothing. Perhaps he is right.

6

Gilg carries the broken man back to his cell. Then I put away the weights and cuffs, tuck his confession into my belt, and douse the small fire. Only then, standing in the dark, nothing but darkness myself, do I notice the sound.

It comes from the small window above me. Someone—no, a great many people are chanting. There is a wild rhythm to their voices, as if they fear God might strike them down before they finish.

Ah yes, I had forgotten about the Brethren.

I leave the Falterkammer in cold darkness, and lock the door carefully. Gilg once tried to pick the lock, that he might drag one of his more hated charges into my workroom to try his hand at the job. I learned of it upon seeing scratchmarks around the lock. And I warned him I would kill him if he tried it again. That is my right, as Scharfrichter. And while he was never so brazen as to take a blade to the lock again, I do not doubt that he checks the door each time after I am gone, in hopes of finding it open.

Now I take another set of stairs, nearer to the cells, up into the Rathaus. I enter into the rear chamber where the Konsultaten keeps his office. It is empty. There is not even a guard on duty outside the door.

I want only to leave the confession with him. The sooner he records it, the sooner I will have some money to give to Tante. She is the only one I trust to go to the Marktplatz and buy provisions. The whores would likely cheat me, and Jorg would be cheated by the merchants. Only Tante, sister of the man who raised me, is honest with my money and shrewd in her haggling with the butchers and farmers.

I, of course, am prohibited from the Marktplatz. The town worries that the Scharfrichter's presence would sour the milk, or spoil the meats.

I turn on my heel, and head for the chambers of the Schoeffen. He does not like to speak to me. It is beneath him. His place is in the elaborate pulpit carved into a wall of the sentencing room, where he can stand in his fine velvets and brocades and frown grandly at the prisoner, pronouncing final sentence. He does not like admitting any connection to the world below the Rathaus, where Gilg and I reign.

Meister Schoeffen is not there either. His two personal guards, always stationed outside his door like the stone gargoyles above the church lintel, never moving, ever watchful, are gone as well.

Then I remember the chanting. The windows are shuttered against the cold, but if I stand still and strain to listen, I can hear the Brethren.

I unfasten leather thongs holding fast a pair of shutters. And I look out onto the Marktplatz to see it more crowded than I have ever witnessed.

Townspeople pack the perimeter, their mass rippling as each tries to get a better view. Meister Schoeffen, the Konsultaten, the guards, and even Gilg, stand on the Rathaus stairs or just within the wall that divides the building's facade from the square. And all of them, from the grand judge to the jailer, are watching a circle of men in the center of the human storm.

It is the source of the chanting. There are over three hundred of them, arranged in small clusters that form a larger circle. Inside the circle stands a man I assume is their leader, for he is surrounded by banner carriers who wave their purple and gold crest in time to the chanting. The leader is not a large man at all. He is bald, without even a marked brow. His cowl and cloak are black, like mine, but with large red crosses sewn on the sleeves and back.

He is swinging a short whip in circles. His followers have thrown back their cowls. They wear black robes with red crosses as well, though not fur-lined like his. Many are barefoot, or wear scraps of shoes. Even from here I can see the sores and blisters.

The men are of all ages, some with broad peasant faces like mine and others with the pinched features of nobility. They stare at their leader.

The chant stops. And mayhem begins.

Like one rabid beast that has broken into many parts, they start tearing at their clothes. They throw off their cloaks and rip open the rags underneath until they are naked to the waist. And they fall to the ground as one, writhing, screaming, moaning.

The leader raises his arms. His back is to me now, and I cannot hear him clearly. He speaks of redemption, of purging the flesh. Then he begins to wade through his followers, stepping over and around them like a haughty merchant picking his way through refuse on a crowded street.

SMACK! The whip slaps down on the back of one man. For what reason, I cannot say. He seemed no different than the others. The leader thrashes another, then another, choosing his victims at whim, it seems.

A low rumble, like far-off thunder, issues from the Brethren. They rise again, and with the leader cracking his whip for time, they pull their own scourges from their belts, and begin flailing themselves. It sounds like the applause that follows an execution.

The townspeople are clapping. They clap in time to the whip, they clap to show approval, perhaps even because they need to do something and can think of nothing else.

Those assembled in front of the Rathaus do not applaud. The guards are restless now, frowning amongst themselves as the Brethren grow more frenzied. Their backs are raw, scars barely healed from their last performance ripped open anew. The pain seems to excite them only more. Some whirl in wild dance as they scourge themselves; others fall to their knees and cry out what sounds like prayer.

I have never seen anything like it.

The leader is facing me now. I do not like the lines of his face. In my work, I must read men quickly and accurately, and decide which course of interrogation I will take. So that is how I know, even from halfway across the Marktplatz, that I am looking at a dangerous man. He is a man who has developed a taste for being followed, for having the power he has over these wretches. He is a man who thinks himself above the law.

One man shrieks louder than the rest. He is beside the leader, on all fours. He has lost his scourge, or thrown it away perhaps. Two others whip him. Already his back is nothing but pulp. He looks like a partly skinned wolf crouching there, with his shaggy black hair. Then I realize he is not shrieking. It is a madman's laughter I hear.

I have no desire to watch any more of this spectacle. I walk outside, down the stairs, coming up behind the Schoeffen and his men. For a man of my size I move quietly. They start in a hare-scared jump at my voice.

"Here is the Jew's confession." I hand over the parchment to the Konsultaten.

They frown but do not meet my eyes. I am supposed to use the front door of the Rathaus only on my way to the Rabenstein.

"Your work is done for today, then?" The Schoeffen speaks to me directly. I am almost too surprised to nod. He looks me up and down, and I wonder what he sees. "Meister Scharfrichter, will you stay here with us for a while?"

"Why?" When have these men, except for Gilg, ever tolerated my company?

The Schoeffen's pale eyes flick back toward the square. "Our visitors. I have heard they can get out of sorts with mischief. We may need help getting them to leave."

I have no wish to stand beside these strangers and watch. Nor is breaking up mischief, should it occur, among the Scharfrichter's duties. I owe the townspeople nothing.

I turn my back and disappear into the Rathaus. I will not police streets I myself am not free to walk.

The town outside the border of the Marktplatz is too quiet for a Saturday noon. Everyone has gone to watch the Brethren. I leave them to their obscene ritual and pass under the old black stockade of the Rabentor, then up the hill and into the trees.

The house is quiet, too. Perhaps the whores and Tante heard the chanting; cold air such as today's carries sound far. Perhaps they went to see for themselves.

Only Gerta is there, sitting in a rocking chair beside a low fire in the hearth. She looks very tired, her skin like paper stretched nearly to tearing. When I enter she looks down at her stockinged feet.

She is Jorg's mother. She had Jorg late for a woman, and against her wishes, I think. She had already given up whoring, unable to draw customers even for the smallest price. Not with Elise in the house. Instead she helped Tante with the chores. She was a very good seamstress as well until her eyes weakened a few years ago. I remember now that she made all of Sabine's dresses, taking too much delight in doing so and creating designs too grand for the daughter of a Scharfrichter. I think again of the blue silk the farmer's daughter gave me last midnight.

I was still young when Gerta grew round with Jorg, and I do not remember how it was that the man who raised me chose her as his permanent bedwarmer. I was old enough when he died, however, to know why she smiled when she heard the news. The working whores could not be beaten too badly, else customers would shy from their bruised faces. But Gerta was at his disposal completely.

"Where are the others?"

"Looking for Sabine."

So, that is what has happened. I wonder if Elise's hysterical tears spurred them to action, or if Jorg recruited them to help on a task he knew he alone could not accomplish. Now I will have tired, complaining women on my hands, and no warm supper.

"You do not care."

I look up as I pull off my boots. Gerta is not one to speak this way to anyone. The man who raised me broke her will along with her jaw and ribs. Elise has been hard at work, stirring them all up.

"She will come back," I mutter, feeling suddenly obliged to say something. "A girl in thin boots such as hers cannot get far in the snow."

Besides, Sabine is clever enough to know there is nothing for her outside my house. I feed her well, clothe her. A day or two out in the cold will remind her who has taken care of her.

"And if she does not?"

I do not answer. To hell with Gerta, with them all. They have it good here. I do not beat them for pleasure, or lock them in the cellar surrounded by beets and darkness on a whim, as happened when the man who raised me was alive.

Sabine will come back. She is my daughter, after all, and although she takes after her mother in the fast shedding of tears, she has my wits.

Gerta says nothing more to me. But her rheumy eyes follow me as I set my boots near the fire to dry and then search in the cupboard for something to eat. There is only a little bread left, and a few small browned apples. And, of course, that damned basket of eggs that the girl brought last night. I think of the blue silk again.

It is hours before they return. Already the sky is turning from gray to red in the west. They are tired, Tante more than the younger ones. I am surprised she went at all, at her age. I can tell by their faces that they have not found her. Jorg is sniffling, but whether it is from the cold or impending tears, I am not sure.

Elise sees me, half-hidden among the trees where I am chopping more wood for the hearth. She marches over, the frosted air turning her beauty into vivid red cheeks and eyes like the heart of a flame.

"She is not in the town. We went from door to door, looking. No one has seen her."

I bring the ax down on a thick piece of trunk. It splits neatly.

"There are men in town, the ones who whip themselves," she continues, when she sees I have no care to make conversation. "What if one of them takes Sabine? They are strange creatures. Who knows what they might do!"

"They are too busy with their ceremony."

"They set the Jewish quarter on fire."

I glance over my shoulder at that. The wind sent the smoke in the wrong direction for me to smell it, but now I can see the Brethren did not restrict themselves to self-punishment. The near corner of the city is shrouded in black smoke, some flames licking at the second floors of buildings. I wonder if the Schoeffen tried to stop them. Likely not, if they confined their mischief to that section of town. Better to sate their lust for destruction at the usurers' expense than have their attentions turn toward the guildhalls or merchants' homes.

Then I see them. They are still several minutes down the trail, but they are walking quickly. Toward us. Three men. In the gloomy light they look like copies of myself, black robes catching on the snow as their boots sink into it. Then they are near enough that I see the red crosses sewn on their cloaks.

"Inside," I mutter, and turn to see Elise has already gone. Jorg and the others are long since inside, boots off already, probably.

I reach the house with barely enough time to put on my mask and send the rest of them into the back room. Already the men are knocking at the door.

It is the Brethren leader and his two banner carriers. From their girth and frowns, I guess that they are also his bodyguards.

"We hear there are women to be had."

I nod, and call for Elise and Claudia over my shoulder. The leader licks his lips, nodding eagerly when I name the price.

"That is for both?"

"No, for each one."

He slurps again. He has a thick, dark tongue that moves like a giant worm in his mouth. When he takes out a coin purse tucked into his trousers, I hear a heavy jingle. He carries no small amount of money for a man who has professed a vow of poverty.

He starts toward them, hands outstretched and eager.

"No, not here." I say it sharply enough to startle him. "There's a room behind the house."

Claudia shows them the way out, head bowed. Elise gives me a look that I think would be effective in extracting confessions in the Falterkammer. It is not the men she is angry over. I know her well enough. She is still upset about Sabine.

Now I am left alone with Jorg and Tante. Gerta has gone to bed already.

"Marcus, will you not look for Sabine with me?" Jorg pleads. When I sit on a bench I have drawn near the hearth, he cowers at my feet. "Please!"

"Now? It's dark." I swipe his hand from my knee.

"She must be so cold, and hungry. I would be scared."

I see the tears welling up in his simple eyes and think, yes, Jorg would be scared. But Sabine is probably holed up somewhere warm and dry, wily thing she is, waiting for all of them to be upset long enough before she returns to collect on their fear for her well-being and subsequent relief.

A thought strikes me then. The lepers who lived in a steep meadow above our house had a barn. They have long since disappeared, either to hell or a better town than ours, but the structure is still there. I wandered past it in summer, and happened upon Sabine playing inside, hanging from its rafters like a bat.

I ask Jorg if he has thought to look there. He shakes his head.

"Well, tomorrow, at first light, you should go look. If she does not come back before then."

"Let's look now!"

"No. You can look tomorrow."

"Please, Marcus—"

I sigh. A glance at Tante tells me she will be long in preparing the evening meal. Her bent fingers are still numb from the cold. She chops a turnip clumsily.

"All right, Jorg. Go ahead. Take a lantern and Hund, if he will go with you."

"Will you not come? I'm afraid to go where lepers have been, in the dark, too."

"It will be cold tonight, Marcus," Tante says, looking up from the turnips. She has been listening all along. "Colder than last night. Cold enough to kill her if she falls asleep."

I have no desire to listen to them for the rest of the night. I pull on my boots, resigned. It will take but an hour to climb up to the barn and back. Whether or not Sabine is there, that is an hour free of their nagging.

7

The abandoned barn looms before us, pale against the dark forest. The lepers built it soundly. Its walls look freshly daubed and I see no gap in the thatched roof, though it is years since anyone maintained it.

The pines are taller here. I feel as if I am growing shorter as I walk, becoming as small and insignificant as Jorg. He pants behind me like the dogs that chase the carriages of nobles.

"Marcus! Slow down! Do not leave me here in the dark!"

I gesture for quiet as he labors through the snow to catch up with me. If Sabine is there, hiding, it will be best to surprise her. Otherwise the half of herself she inherited from Elise may get the foolish notion to run off into the snows.

The door is unlatched and open slightly. I hold my lantern up to the crack and peek inside. There is only darkness beyond a narrow orange slice of light thrown by the lantern. If she is there, and not yet ready to be found, she will make a dash for it. I throw open the door and rush inside.

Jorg is at my heels. He screams.

The shadows overhead, where ceiling and support beams meet, are alive in a swaying mass of black and gray. Bats, hundreds of them deep in the wintersleep of their kind.

Jorg is afraid of bats. He is afraid of spiders, too, and the rats and mice that move about the house at night.

He runs from the barn and into the night. Probably he will run all the way back to the house.

Other than the bats, the barn is empty. Cobwebs and droppings cover its dirt floor. If Sabine thought to hide here, she did not stay long.

Then I see it.

It is just at the edge of the door. I missed it in my rush to surprise the girl I thought was inside. A sharp splinter of wood along the frame caught a piece of fabric. The small shred of green wool matches Sabine's work dress. And it is newly there, not a remnant from her summer exploring.

I glance down in the snow and see a third set of footprints. It has not snowed in three days, and the powder that is left is dry. It takes a cast of a foot nicely. So, Sabine did come to the barn. The tracks lead farther up the hill, into the trees. There is nothing beyond the old lepers' meadow but forest. There are no roads for miles.

Perhaps I was wrong to think she was clever. Only a fool would run off in that direction.

Tomorrow, I decide suddenly. It is too dark now to do much tracking, but tomorrow is the Sabbath. The priest does not wish to see me at Mass, but all the others will be there. The Rathaus and everything in it, and below it, enjoy a day of rest. I will come back tomorrow and follow those tracks, to see where the spoiled girl has gone.

When I find her, she will learn not to run off again and leave me with anxious, nagging women.

By the time I return to the house, Elise and Claudia have finished with the men. The Brethren are nowhere to be seen. Good. I have no desire to let them into my home, to drink and speak of foolishness, as some of the whores' visitors seem to expect of me.

Jorg is still trembling, telling and retelling anyone who will listen to him prattle on about the bats. Elise and Claudia say nothing. They are in a bad humor, both of them. Tante is as well. They must still be unsettled over Sabine.

The stew is thin tonight, more melted snow than anything else. I give Tante the Brethren's coins. It will be enough to buy some good provisions, though she will have to wait until after the Sabbath to go to market.

I fish out a piece of boiled egg from my bowl and feed it to Hund, who sits beside me patiently. I find another piece. And another.

The stew is a waste. I set aside my bowl full of more eggs and bits of grubby turnip. The others ignore me and eat in silence. I do not mind. At least Jorg has stopped reciting his tale.

Claudia is nearest me. Either the cold or her time with the men, perhaps both, has turned her cheeks bright and warm. She feels my eyes on her and glances up.

"Come to my room when you finish."

I leave them then. Hund trots at my feet down the hall to my room. He watches from my doorway as I light a small lamp. But I wave him off. There will be no room in my bed for a large dog. He slinks back down the hall, likely to finish my bowl of eggs.

Claudia takes her time in joining me. Even after I open the door and wave her through, she lingers in the hall. Pressing her lips together, as if in some decision, she enters my room and shuts the door.

I am already naked but for a thin pair of breeches I wear under my blood-stained woolen trousers. She sits on the bed and slips off her dress quickly, staring at the floor.

She has none of Elise's seductive charms. But then Elise, who teases me when she undresses but is just as quick to bite or scratch, is too unpredictable for me at times. Claudia knows what to do, and does it without complaint.

She lies back on the bed, staring at the ceiling.

I am surprised. She knows my tastes. "Roll over."

"Do you not want me facing you, for once?" she asks too quickly, trying to give me a pretty smile. She is nervous about something.

"Roll over."

She does, turning on all fours with her head bowed in shame.

Her back is a pattern of bloody stripes. Now that she has moved I see they have stained my pillow. I kneel over her and frown.

"The Brethren did this?"

She nods. "And no better to Elise. They said we must repent for being wicked."

I mutter under my breath. The men ought not mistreat them. It is disrespectful to me. I wonder if either she or Elise called out as it happened. Had I been in the house, and not on a search for a troublesome girl, I might have heard them.

"It is no matter," she says suddenly. She glances over her shoulder and sees my mood has changed. Pulling on her dress, she speaks quickly. I can tell she is repeating the words Elise gave her.

"Do not be angry that you did not hear us. At first we did not understand why you did not come when we cried out, but then afterward Tante told us. It is good that you went looking for Sabine. That is most important."

Sabine, Sabine. I am starting to hate the sound of her name. I leave her then, sitting on my bed, and go to my coffer beside the hearth. There is just enough of the sweet-smelling Beinwell to make poultice for both of them. Bleeding as they are, the women are of no use in either chores or whoring. I will need to mend them.

I spread the mash across their wounds and wrap cloth tightly around their torsos, so that the poultice will not rub off against their beds in the night. Elise grabs my hand as it passes over her breast and holds it there. I glance up at her.

Her lips are suddenly hard against mine, her tongue forcing my mouth open. As my skills are in the Falterkammer, and at healing wounds, so are hers in areas more advantageous for a whore.

"Thank you for looking for her. You'll start again tomorrow, at dawn, yes? I know you can find her."

She tries to kiss me again, but I turn my face. She need not mention Sabine's name to worsen my mood.

I finished tending to them and send them to bed. I am of a mind to go into town and find the Brethren leader, punish him for his wanton act, and let all those who would copy him know I do not allow such abuse of my whores.

But such thoughts are futile. There is no point in another long walk in the cold, down to the town and along the few streets where I am allowed, searching for a man who is probably fast asleep, drunk and with a full belly, under some warm blanket in a guest room.

I fall asleep hunched on the bench before the hearth, and dream of nothing.

8

"Meister Scharfrichter!"

The men's shouts jolt me awake. As I stand up from the bench, my back creaks like the rope pulley in the Falterkammer. Dawn light and cold leak in through cracks in the leather shutters.

I am confused. It is the morning of the Sabbath. Men such as the ones outside my door ought to be in church.

The Schoeffen's guards have come. I throw on my mask and open the door even as they pound against it. What would bring them here, so early, and on the Sabbath, close enough to touch me? These are men who wash their cloaks whenever I brush against them in the Rathaus.

"What is it?"

They are surprised by the sight of me, bare-chested and bare-footed, sunless skin all the paler against my black hood and trousers. But they recover their wits fast enough.

"The Brethren are gone. The Council met last night, and decided to force them out," sputters the younger guard. Sweat pours down his ruddy, blunt-featured face. I wonder again what would make them run through the snow to my home, these two whom I have never seen move swifter than a cloud on a windless day.

"So?"

"There was trouble. Some of the Brethren, ones who instigated the burning of the Jews, were still not sated. No one could find the man who leads them, to urge them on to the next town." This from the older guard, father to the first. They are near twins in appearance, despite the difference in years.

"So?"

"They got into more mischief. Smashed a window at the weavers' guild. Tried to set fire to the church—"

The younger one interrupts. He has gotten his breath back. “A few of them got loose into some of the homes, including that of Meister Schoeffen. To rob them, we thought. Until we discovered his daughter missing, and her maidservant as well.”

Now I understand the panic in their eyes. Ah, to be the Schoeffen’s bodyguards and lose track of his most beloved offspring, the only girl among seven children and the center of his universe. But I do not see why they have come for me.

“By the time we learned of her disappearance, the Brethren leader had returned, and all of us had run them out. Then, this morning, searching for her, we found one of the wretches.”

“And?” I am getting cold, standing with no shirt in front of winter winds.

The pair of them exchange glances. The father speaks first. “He was one of the wilder ones, to be sure. We found him on a roadside, doing unspeakable things with the corpse of a dead girl.”

“Violating her,” adds the younger one, as if I could not guess as much. He shrinks back from my glare.

“Who was the girl?”

They shrug as one unit. “Don’t know. Didn’t recognize her. Some wench they picked up along the way, likely. But we’re sure he knows where Meister Schoeffen’s daughter is. Gilg has him now. We need you to...speak with him.”

Ah, so there it is. My naked feet are nearly frozen to the cold earthen floor of my house. I nod, wondering if I can charge more for working on the Sabbath. Another thought wanders across my mind.

“The girl, the one who was killed. You saw her then?”

They nod. “Some of the other guards took her body to the church, to see if anyone recognized her.”

“And...” Suddenly the cold pinches shut my throat. I cough to clear it. “And what did she look like?”

“Not much left to see,” mutters the young one. He glances to his father for confirmation.

The older man shrugs. “Young, it looks like. Reddish hair, I think. More than that I couldn’t say. The brute who killed her took a knife to her.”

“Was she wearing...” I cough again. “The dress, was it green?”

“There was no dress when we found her.”

I nod. I close the door in their faces, knowing better than to invite them inside. No man, unless looking for a cure or a whore, cares to enter the Scharfrichter's home. No one else is awake yet. Good. I do not want them down here as I dress, asking me if I am going to find Sabine. Perhaps I am.

"Marcus, I heard voices." Jorg yawns as he enters the room.

"Come, we are going to work." He will be useful to me. He is only the Loewe, not Scharfrichter, and is free to enter the church if he chooses. He can see if he recognizes the nameless girl.

Even as I decide this, and hasten him to pull on his boots, I am thinking. Sabine did not go to town often. Hers might not be a face known to the guards. But it could be some other girl, even the Schoeffen's child, unrecognizable if the wounds inflicted were severe enough.

I throw open the door and send the Schoeffen's guards skittering off the porch.

They run alongside Jorg to catch up with my long strides in the snow, down the hill, toward the Falterkammer.

"Jorg!" I call for him over my shoulder as we pass under the Rabentor. He nearly stumbles in a sudden sprint to join me. "Go to the church. The body of a girl is there. Tell me if it is Sabine."

His mouth works, mind running over what I have said once, twice. His lips curl back in horror. "But, Sabine! What, what will I do if it is?"

"Come back to the jail and tell me." I had thought this would be a simple task for him.

"No!" The tears bubble up suddenly and fiercely, a flash flood spilling over onto his cheeks. "No, she cannot be dead, no, it cannot be."

His voice cracks and splinters into unintelligible sobbing. He will not go.

I look down at his child's tears with frustrated pity. It is just as well. I doubt in his sudden state of wretchedness that he would recognize Sabine.

The whole of the jail is brightly lit this time. Meister Schoeffen stands at the foot of the stairs, pacing, wringing his hands. When he sees me, he lets out a small cry of relief. He has never welcomed me before.

Gilg has been waiting in the shadows. And then I am glad again to lock the door to my workroom so carefully. With all these men so eager, I do not doubt that the wretch they found would be strung up over my hearth and of no use to anyone by now if they had gained access to the Falterkammer.

Like one of the earthen jail walls come alive, Gilg steps forward and grunts at me.

"Go get him, then."

He stomps off. His footsteps are heavy not in anger, but simply from his weight. I feel the walls shake a little.

As I unlock the door to the Falterkammer, I am aware that not only Jorg is behind me. The guards are there, and Meister Schoeffen. Their combined apprehension gives off a sharp, acrid smell in the narrow space.

"You can wait upstairs."

Meister Schoeffen shoves at Jorg as the door swings inward, into darkness. "No, it is my daughter that is missing. I must bear witness."

I stand in such a way that my bulk prevents any of them from passing over the threshold of the Falterkammer, my workroom. "My work is best done without distraction. You and your men can continue the search, or go to church and pray."

Meister Schoeffen does not like the tone in my voice. I can see his mind forming a remark to put me in my place. Then he remembers this is my place. It is here, in the dungeons below his fine offices, that I am the one in charge.

"I will stay. Let the guards leave to search the forest again. They can bring me news. I will say nothing, and be like a statue in the corner."

I glance at the guards and see they are eager for me to agree. Then I remember they are not in the Schoeffen's good graces at the moment, having let madmen steal his daughter from her bed. They would not be unhappy without his company.

It is too late to discuss this further. Gilg is coming, carrying the prisoner over his shoulder at an angle that makes the man's head slam against the wall with every step. The big man cannot enter unless the others move into the room. And the prisoner is near enough already to hear what I say. He must not have the impression that my authority is anything less than total here.

"You, stand there, and you two, leave us." I glower at Meister Schoeffen for complicating matters as I light the room's small hearth.

Gilg throws the man onto the floor. Then he steps back, waiting. They are all waiting, including the wretch staring up at me. I let them wait.

I stand over the prisoner's head, hands on my hips, and stare back at him. He must think I am twice my already looming height from his position. Good.

I recognize him at once. He is the wolfish, shaggy-haired member of the Brethren who wailed louder than all the rest during their spectacle yesterday. He is the one who fell on all fours in front of the leader, begging not to be spared the whip. I look into his dark eyes and see a madman. He is the kind of man who likes pain, both dispensing and incurring it. I will allow him neither.

"Stand up."

He does not move. He is very thin, long in the limb, but frail. His skin has a gray pallor to it.

Then he grins at me. His angular face turns into a leering skull. "Try to kill me."

I hear Meister Schoeffen mutter off to one side. A talking statue, then. Damn him.

"Stand up first."

"The pale horseman is coming for you." He smiles again. His mouth is a black hole of rot. "He rides toward you even now."

I bend down and grab his shirt, twisting it for a better hold. And then I lift him, not just to his feet but beyond, so his eyes are level with mine. I hold him there, his scrawny legs swaying above the floor. He does not struggle.

His eyes are inches from the hooked nose of my mask. There is a cloudiness to his stare, as if he is drunk or fevered.

"Where are the maids the Brethren stole from their beds last night?"

His laugh is like the screech of bats. Suddenly he stops, sucking in air as if I were choking him. He starts to cough.

It is a deep cough, with a rattle to it that I have never heard. Phlegm spews from his mouth. I see flecks of blood dribbling down his chin.

Then he raises his head. And spits. The gob of phlegm hits the brow of my mask. Some of it drips down into my eye.

"You are dead, you are dead," he sings.

I bring him closer to me, so close that he turns his cheek to avoid being stabbed by the sharp end of the mask's nose. "No. I am Death."

This gives him pause. His eyes dart over me. There is madness still behind them, but now I see intelligence as well. He spits again.

I let him drop as if he were a sack of flour that suddenly became too heavy. And I turn my back. I do not care to let him see me wipe off the spittle. Knowing he is still in a heap behind me, I gesture to Gilg and Jorg.

They each grab one of his arms, and fasten the cuffs tightly. I hear all this, my back still turned. And I hear the man spitting. He does not protest, though I am sure Gilg is not being gentle with him. Only he spits.

Meister Schoeffen has edged nearer, eyes narrowed. He ignores me as I watch him creep ever closer. I can see in his eyes he is as eager for a confession as he is for blood. One of the man's lobs smacks him in the nose and he steps back.

Slowly I heat a pair of tongs over low flames, partly turned toward my charge so that he can see what I am doing. He laughs again.

"Absolution, absolution!" he howls, throwing his head back and rattling his restraints. "There must be absolution before the pale horseman arrives!"

The ends of the tongs are glowing a hot red, like a sunset. Like fresh blood. Like Sabine's hair, I think suddenly, and my own.

It is bad to be thinking this way. It is wrong. I am here to ask questions, to extract truth. I can think of these other things later.

"I ABSOLVE YOU!" The man's sudden scream fades in a wheeze. He coughs again, hard, wet coughs that spray spittle and blood on Jorg and myself, the two nearest him.

He is looking at the tongs. When the coughing fades, he smiles again. He wants to feel their heat, I can tell. In his madness he longs for them to sear his flesh and cleanse him. So I will stand here, idly turning the tongs over the flames though they are already hot enough. It is the waiting for him that is unbearable.

"You will tell me what you know of Meister Schoeffen's daughter, the one you and your Brethren stole in the night. Where is she?"

He sputters something I do not understand. His lungs clear long enough for him to repeat himself. "Do you mean the pretty whore we found, wandering? She needed absolution from the pale horseman."

I repeat the question. It is good I am wearing the mask. He cannot see the tightness in my jaw.

"Sting me," he whispers. He licks his lips, watching the tongs. "Do it!"

I look at him directly. "No. First you will answer my question."

He whimpers like a dog denied its bone.

I hear them coming moments before they burst into my workroom. It is the father and son guards.

"She is found, Meister Schoeffen!" They cry as one, grinning. "Fraulein is at home, with not a scratch upon her!"

"Praise the Lord Jesus Christ!" The Schoeffen claps his hands together.

The prisoner starts laughing and coughing at once.

"How is it this miracle happened?" Jorg asks this, he who knows full well not to speak in the Falterkammer unless I direct him. The wretch laughs harder, and spits at me again. He knows I am no longer master here. Damn all of them.

"Never mind," says the father guard brusquely. Jorg and I are no longer needed. We are to fade silently into the shadows.

"And what of this man now?" I ask, sharply enough that the rest all stop chattering and stare at me.

Meister Schoeffen waves dismissively. "Take him back to his cell, Meister Lockwirt. We do not need a confession to pass judgment. The guards were witness to his acts against the dead girl."

"And what of that dead girl?" I step between Gilg and the spitting, coughing, wheezing worm of a man.

"Patience, Scharfrichter. You will have your way with the man soon enough, at the Rabenstein. I am going home to my daughter."

"To the whore!" shouts my charge with sudden energy. "To the whore in velvets and furs, slipping out through the gates while the pale horseman burned down the homes of the baby-eating Jews and absolved even those godless insects, the whore with the pretty black hair and her white-browed maid no less comely, slip slip slip away in the night no one sees but I who was to absolve them!"

All of us are listening now. Fraulein Schoeffen has hair black as a raven's wing. Her pale-haired maid is very fair.

"What do you say?" Meister Schoeffen steps back from the door.

"Never mind," mutters the father guard, suddenly anxious. He knows, and now I begin to know, to understand, what happened.

"Your whore-daughter, leaving your house by the back gate, leaving it open so that we may slip slip slip inside and absolve those within. But it was others who did this. Her I followed, her to absolve, watching her shhh! quiet in slippered feet too fine to touch the snow, move through the night to the man's horse, lover's horse, fornicator's horse it is I who should have the horse, not he, for I travel absolving all on a pale horse, but I am without a horse—"

I lose the last of the ramble. It is muffled by his coughing. But I have heard enough to know. In the confusion of the night, knowing her father and the guards were rounding up the Brethren, Fraulein Schoeffen met with a secret lover. Perhaps she meant to be back before dawn, but was delayed. Perhaps she had to hide from the very parties that searched through cold dawn fog and forest for her.

Meister Schoeffen understands now, too. The guards stare at their boots.

"Her I meant to absolve, so I followed them in the night, but the man had a horse and I, the horseman, had no horse." The wretch is lucid again as he speaks. A pink stream of bloody spit drips from one corner of his mouth. "I fell behind, slip slip slip in the snow. I would freeze but for the angel-faced whore that comes along the road, stumbling. Her meat warmed me."

"Put the tongs to the bastard," hisses Meister Schoeffen. His face is as red as the heated irons. "Put the tongs to him and have him tell all. I want to know the name of this rider who meets my child at midnight for seductions. And if not the name then the manner and build of him, and the horse, so that I may find him."

I shake my head. There are too many people in the room, and none of them listening to me. Let those who do not belong here leave me alone with the man, and then I will ask my questions, my way.

Meister Schoeffen frowns when I say this. He grabs a second pair of tongs I had heating in the flames.

He stabs the man in the gut. They scream as one, in surprise, in anger, in delight. The Schoeffen lunges again, but I haul him off and throw him into the corner. Office or no, he has violated the rules of the Falterkammer.

The wretch's body arches away from me, writhing, exalted in the pain. For an instant, I see something under his torn sleeve. It must have been a trick of the shadows.

"Feuer!"

Jorg is at my side with the torch. I rip open what is left of the sleeve and hold the flame close to his armpit, to be sure of what I think I have seen. The man cringes from the heat. Gilg leans into him, holding him steady. He spits again.

"I am the horseman! The pale horseman!"

I pull aside the hairs in the crease of his underarm, to be sure. By now the others have seen it. They gasp as one.

The man's underarm is swollen with black bubbles of infection, some the size of eggs.

"The plague!" screams one of the guards. The others take up the chorus.

"Wait!" I shout at them, even as they back away. They break as one, like a herd that has scented the wolf. Even Jorg and Gilg abandon me.

"Wait, don't run out!" My warning goes unheard. I hear their panicked feet on the stairs. They run out into the morning, into the cold, into the town.

They say one stricken with plague has only to look at another and wish death upon him. If that is true, then we are all dead.

I glance back at the prisoner, his head hung low, arms strained nearly from their sockets. He lifts his head. Now I see how sunken his eyes are, how jaundiced the skin. With or without my ministrations here in the Falterkammer, he will be dead by nightfall. It is this pathetic slip of a madman who brought the plague to us. And who killed a girl, one that could be Sabine.

"The girl." He smiles again. He is looking at me as if with the evil eye. As if he knows what I am thinking. "I wanted only to absolve her, to send her to heaven before the pale horseman came. But she begged me. She begged me to rut her like the whore she was—"

I club him across the collarbone with my fist. His whole body jerks from the impact.

I strike again. And again. And again. I cannot hit him hard enough or fast enough to suit my rage.

One of his bony wrists slips through the cuffs from the force of my blows. He dangles like a child's puppet, his shoulder twisting more violently with each punch.

And I cannot stop. His other hand slips through and he crumples to the floor. I am on my knees, beating what is now nothing but a sack of broken bones. I stand, but only to rest my arms. And I kick. One of the few teeth left to him flies across the room and lands with a sizzle in my hearth.

I bend over, hands on knees, and find I am quaking.

The bells toll then. All the bells of the church sound at once, violently.

They say that the plague flies on stale air, and that the stir of bells can kill it. I do not know this to be true, nor do I care. The bells are calling to me for another purpose.

I leave what is left of my prisoner in a bloody mess. I do not lock the Falterkammer door behind me. I am in too much of a rush to the church, and the body lying within it.

9

The townspeople stream out of the church and into the Marktplatz like the sheep they are. Thoughtless, lacking will other than as one flock, running for their homes in panic.

Some of them even bump into me as they flee. They recoil, faces drawn taut like a bow. The bells do not stop ringing.

"Meister Scharfrichter!" Father Hans sees me on the threshold of his sacred nave. He is standing at the far end, flanked by Meister Schoeffen and his guards. They are all sweating despite the chill given off by the church stones.

"It is forbidden!" He waves me away.

I care little for the rules he and the others devised to restrict the Scharfrichter. I want only to see the girl, to know.

He shouts something else, but I do not hear as I head toward a shadowed chapel off one side of the nave. I shove aside the last stragglers as they race for a safety that has already been lost.

None of them stops to look at her. I doubt that any would have, even without the plague bells clanging overhead. Perhaps a few might have drawn back the shroud out of curiosity, and then continued on their way, gloating a little that their own daughters were safe at home.

Someone covered her with an old shroud and left her lying on the ground, at the feet of the Virgin. The statue looks down at her with unfeeling, wooden eyes. Even she does not care.

As I near I see that blood has soaked through in places on the shroud. She must have been freshly killed when they found her. I can tell from the lay of the shroud that she has been mutilated, breasts cut off, the gut split open.

I stand over her, but cannot bring myself to kneel and lift the shroud. I do not want to see my own gray-green eyes staring up at me.

At last I crouch. I sit on my heels. It is better that way. It does not feel like penance then, before the expressionless Virgin.

I draw back the shroud and stare down at what was once the face of a young maid. The Schoeffen's men were right. There is little left. The man who wielded the knife was thorough. I am spared the sight of my own eyes, lifeless and unfocused. There are no eyes at all.

I am glad that I killed the man who did this, and that I killed him as I did, lacking any mercy. Beheading, even a hanging or breaking him on the wheel, would have been too good for him.

And I cannot but be glad as well to stare at the faceless girl, and know not from her shredded features but from the bright gold curls that frame them. It is not Sabine.

10

Jorg ran home, of course.

Where Gilg went, I do not know. I imagine that, after conferring with the priest, Meister Schoeffen retired to his handsome home, to embrace his precious daughter and then demand to learn of her whereabouts and company the night before.

But Jorg ran through the snow as fast as his scrawny legs could carry him. He did not even mind the trail. I see his tracks as I leave town myself. He plowed across snowbanks in a panic, falling more than once.

Hund is whining on the porch. He jumps up at me, nervous. I do not blame him. Still several feet from my door, I can hear the shrieks within.

They are all there, in the front room. Tante slumps on the bench. Jorg wails at her feet like a toddler denied its blanket. Elise, red-rimmed eyes blazing, is the first to acknowledge me.

"You bastard! Sabine is dead, and now the plague has come!" She jumps to her feet to attack me.

"Sabine is not dead. It was a different girl." I say this loud enough so that all of them hear through their tears and sobbing. "And though a man with plague has been in our town, none of us are yet sick. All of you mourn and scare the dog for nothing."

It is more than I have said to any of them in a long while. They quiet, and stare.

I push past them, to my room. I am hot, as if with fever. Fever is the first sign of plague, say the merchants who talk to Jorg of its devious ways. Now they will talk of the plague coming to our town.

My hood of office lands on the bed. Blood covers my shirt, blood and spittle from the man I left on the floor of the Falterkammer.

I remember then that I did not lock my workroom. I did not even close the door. Gilg will find it wide open and inviting when he returns. If he returns.

I pull off my shirt and throw it outside my room, into the hall. Tante will wash it for me. I have no other, but it is warm enough in the house. I do not want to wear the spittle of the man who called himself the pale horseman.

For a moment I remember the pale horseman's other crime, the evidence lying still and forgotten beneath a bloody shroud. It was not Sabine. For that I am relieved. But still Sabine has not returned. And now, if she does come back, it will be to a place where the plague has been.

Ah, listen to me. I whine and wring my hands worse than Tante. All the women's crying has gotten to me. I call for one of them to fetch and clean the shirt I have thrown into the hall, and then close the door. The morning has tired me, after a night when sleep came poorly. I strip off my trousers and notice they are bloody, too. Not badly enough to call for a washing, especially in this cold. They are of a thick wool, and in such weather would not dry for days. I leave them in a pile at the foot of the bed and crawl beneath the covers.

Hund, who slunk into my room in his quiet way before I shut the door, makes a bed of the trousers and snuffles contentedly. I am wondering what dogs like him dream of as I drift into a heavy slumber.

11

It is already dark when I hear the voice.

She must have begun in a whisper, raising her voice a little each time I did not reply. By the time I wake, I can hear the creak of an old woman's frustration in it.

"Marcus!"

I bid her enter. Tante opens the door, but stays in the hall. There is only enough light to make out her gray outline against the darker gloom.

"Jorg."

She says nothing more. As she stands there in silence, and I do not stir from my bed, I become aware of another sound. It is the breath of a person restless in slumber.

I throw off the covers and push Hund away from the bed he made of my trousers. They are barely above my hips when I am out in the hall, following her to the front room.

Here someone has lit a single, feeble candle. It shines pale yellow light on Jorg's face and makes the sweat on his cheeks glisten. He lies stretched on the length of the bench. There is a hollow sound to his breath as he sleeps.

"How long has he been like this?" I stoop beside him, watching his eyelids flutter. Heat radiates from his fevered flesh. He stirs and whimpers.

Tante tucks a blanket around his shoulder.

"He said lying in bed gave him nightmares," she whispers. "I heard him at the cupboard an hour ago, looking for garlic."

"Garlic?"

She glances up at me. Her eyes look moist. "The merchants told him it keeps away the plaguewalker."

The merchants' tales again.

Some say the plague is a bad walker, a crippled demon. It needs to be carried on the back of its servant, a black giant who strides from town to town, his head higher than the roofs of houses soon to be filled with the dead. Others say the plaguewalker appears as a fair maid, all in red. Or all in white. Sometimes a mix of both.

I think of the black giant and frown at Jorg's twitching features.

Pulling open his shirt, I slip my hand under his arm. There is nothing there but the sweat of a fever. Nor do I feel anything behind his ears. These are the places where the black blisters form, they say.

"Have we garlic?"

Tante nods. "Some. Not much. I planned to buy more at market tomorrow."

"Give him some, if that is what he wants."

"Can you offer him nothing?" Her anxious eyes dart to the coffer where I keep my herbs.

"No." I straighten and make for my room. A brew made with dried Scharfgarbe leaves would help one sweat out fever, but I do not consider them for Jorg. He is sweating too much already.

"Marcus..." Her voice fades, leaving unsaid the plea I can sense. She wants, no, expects me to do something.

I glance at her over my shoulder, on her old knees beside Jorg like a penitent at the altar. "I doubt it is the plague, Tante, else I would be ill as well. Likely Jorg worked himself into a fever from fear."

I do not wait for her to answer. If she does I do not hear it.

Again I sleep poorly. It is not like me to waste time meant for slumber. Nor do I usually dream. But tonight is different. I have heard Jorg repeat too many of the merchants' tales.

I dream of the plaguewalker.

In my dream it is not a black giant bearing a cripple on its back. Instead it shows itself in its other form, the plague maiden.

She walks ahead of me, on a snowy trail. My own black cloak drags over the snow as I hurry to catch up with the her. My legs feel heavy, as if with fever.

I am almost to the plague maiden, her red cloak like blood staining the white of winter, when she turns and looks at me with my own pale eyes.

Sabine's face fades with the dream. It is just dawn, the first gray of day filtering through an oiled hide I have tacked over the room's narrow, glassless window. I do not like to keep my room shuttered, even in winter. Closed up, it smells and looks too much like the Falterkammer. I spend enough time there.

I get up and dress but for my shirt, which I hope Tante has not forgotten to wash. It is warm in the hall when I open my door. Someone stoked the hearth fire all night.

Jorg is still on the bench, face to the wall. The women sit near him except for Tante. She stands at the door, wrapping a scarf over her unplaited hair.

Gerta coughs suddenly. All but Jorg turn to stare at her, startled. Then they look at me.

I am already among them, leaning over Jorg. He rolls toward me suddenly.

His face is swollen, so pale it is almost blue. His eyes are bloodshot. And his breath rattles like a handful of coins in a cage. The fever still rages.

Gerta coughs again.

I look up and realize it is not she who coughed, but Claudia. They are all nervous now, except for Jorg. He is beyond nervous.

Again I feel for blisters under his arms. There are none.

"I am going to market, Marcus," Tante says quietly. "Have you anything to add to the list you gave me?"

Her eyes look wet, but not with tears. She is afraid.

"Ask if anyone else has been taken with so strong a fever."

She nods, and leaves. Hund follows her out into the snow.

Jorg sits up suddenly and grabs my shoulder, nearly knocking me off my heels. He coughs violently, so hard that veins stand out purple against his pale flesh. Sputum and blood spray out in all directions.

He cannot breathe. He tries to take in air but cannot. I feel his fingernails dig into my skin as his mouth works furiously, trying to force in air. With a terrible sucking noise his whole body jerks. He falls backward onto the bench, wheezing.

"He has been that way since midnight," growls an unfamiliar voice behind me.

It is Elise, her own throat constricted. She is looking at me with very wide eyes.

"Have all of you a fever?"

They glance among themselves, as if it is a secret to which I should not be privy. And then they nod.

I sit back on my heels and stare at Jorg. He starts to cough again.

"It is good Sabine ran away before the plague came."

I can barely hear Elise over Jorg's sputtering.

THUD THUD THUD. Someone knocks at the door, not furtively, but with authority and anger. I get up to look for my mask.

The women do not move. They sit with heads bowed, hands idle in their laps. Already they act like weepers at Jorg's grave. I notice my shirt, clean and folded on the arm of Gerta's chair, and pull it on along with my hood.

It is half of the Schoeffen's personal guard. It is the father come. His son is likely behind with their charge, or perhaps guarding the wayward daughter.

"Meister Scharfrichter!" He steps back to the edge of the porch when I open the door. He is holding a scroll in his hand, sealed with the dark red wax of the council. I wonder what they have decreed that would need my notice.

He throws the scroll at me and stumbles backward down the stairs in his rush to leave. I watch him half-run, half-flail in the deep snow, toward town.

The style of the words is more courtly than from my hand, but I can read the message well enough to understand it, and be angry.

They are fining me, and think I should be grateful for it. I was seen crossing the Marktplatz yesterday, and then daring to defile the church with my presence. Half the town was witness to it. And it was after my transgressions that God chose to visit the plague upon the town, punishing them all for my sin. I should be thankful it is only a fine of coin, though a heady one at that. They need not remind me what happened to the last Scharfrichter when he failed in his duties.

I frown at the vellum, but not because of the fine. The plague has indeed come, then. Others must be sick as well, else the council would not have written it so. I glance at Jorg. The terrible choking rhythm of his coughs does not cease.

I do not remember coughing in all his tales of the plague. I remember hearing of black boils and madness from the pain, but nothing of coughing. Perhaps I did not listen well enough.

The women want to know what is writ on the scroll. I tell them. They mutter as one.

"They would blame it on us."

"That much silver you'll not earn in all the year. How will you pay it?"

"Bastards."

Jorg sits up again. He tries to stand, but topples over and falls on Elise. I pick him up and try to set him down again, but he will not have it. He squirms and flails. The drool streaming from his slack lips is naught but blood.

His mouth makes a gobbling motion, greedy for air. He is crying now, but from pain or fear I cannot say. At last he slumps forward. I catch him, and feel the heaviness in his slight body.

"We will put him in his bed," I announce. Then I sling him over my shoulder and carry him back down the hall, up the ladder stairs to the top of the house. His room is barely big enough for his bed, and it is not a full bed at that. Just a thick bedroll, lumped and stained with age. Here he and I slept when we were younger. I have not been in this room for years.

I stoop to pass under the lintel and lay him down. He is still limp. Only a weak rattle of breath tells me he is alive.

The women follow me up the stairs, like a funeral procession. Elise and Claudia stay at the landing. Gerta slips in after me, and curls up at the foot of the bed.

"I will stay with him," she murmurs. Sometimes I forget she is his mother. To her he must be more than a chattering simpleton. I nod and leave them.

I cannot sit idly in the front room, with Elise and Claudia swallowing each cough as if to pretend they are not ill. I pull on my boots and cloak.

But I do not head for the town. Instead I climb higher, past the lepers' old field, past the barn full of bats asleep and unaware that the plague has come. I walk here often to search for my plants in welcome solitude. It is quiet, and always cool, even in summer. The pines shade the trail. Now, in winter, it is frigid. The bitter air feels good as it fills my lungs. It tells me I can still breathe.

I did not intend to follow her footprints. They are still readable, for it has not snowed since before she left. She has big feet for a girl, I think to myself as I trace her path up into the hills. I wonder if she came this way at night. She is braver than I thought. Or more foolish. No, a fool would not have the courage to wander here in the darkness. She was brave, and determined.

I am gone for most of the morning, walking the path she took when she fled my house. The trail crosses an old, rutted road that skirts around low mountains and then heads north. But the way has not been used for years, since the day the whole earth shook down one of the mountains that loomed over it. A few miles along, the road is buried in rock and debris. It is not passable for horses and wagons.

But Sabine did not know that. Perhaps she did but did not care. A wily young creature like her could scramble over the fallen rock, risking only some scratches and a torn hem.

Her footprints turn onto the road, toward the rockslide. I follow them. It gives me something to do.

I reach the remains of the fallen mountain at noon, already more than half a day from home. If I clamber up onto the slippery, icy rubble, it will take at least an hour to reach the other side. And then what? I will be that much farther from my bed.

I follow her path with my eyes. Her footprints zigzag up the jumble of snow-covered rocks and then disappear over the crest.

She was determined to flee. Better an uncertain future, or none at all, than to marry a Scharfrichter.

I stand too long there, staring at the bootprint near my foot. She has big feet for a girl.

At last I turn my back on the fallen mountain, and use my long legs to their fullest. I will not be home before nightfall.

12

He is dead.

I know it as I near the house. How, I cannot say. I feel it in my gut. Jorg is dead.

The look on Tante's face when I enter tells me I am right. The tears are gone already. All of them are silent, except for the coughing.

"He is in his bed." Gerta says this. I can see she wishes to say more, but shakes her head, as if reproaching herself. The man who raised me taught her with the back of his hand, and sometimes his boot, that it is better to be silent.

They are all so pale. Even Elise looks frail.

"I found the trail Sabine took," I announce. They will be pleased to know she did not freeze the first night of her flight as they feared.

Elise gasps at this. She stares up at me. I did not expect to see terror in her eyes.

"Please, Marcus, leave her alone. Do not look for her. I do not want her to suffer like this."

The others look away, too quickly, when I glance at them. They are all thinking it. I was the one closest to the man who brought plague to our town. And yet I am well. I stare hard at Tante, until she raises her eyes to meet mine.

"In town, in the market, there are others sick?"

She nods. When she opens her mouth to speak, there is nothing but a wheeze. Forming the sound into words makes her frown in pain. "Meister Schoeffen and his family. His young guard Martin is already dead. Many are as we, and still more are fleeing before they fall ill."

"You should all rest." It is more a command than a suggestion. There is nothing they can do sitting here in the front room. And there is no need for them to see me taking out my shovel to dig a grave for Jorg.

Gerta and the younger ones shuffle off to their rooms. Tante stays. She is not finished with me yet.

"Marcus." She pauses to force more precious air into her lungs. It is like working a bellows that has been stoppered. Now I see that her eyes are glazed not with fear or tears, but fever. I sit next to her on the bench and notice how thin her legs are beside mine.

"The end for Jorg was very bad," she whispers. It is as if the cough has fallen asleep and she dares not rouse it. "He was in terrible pain. Gerta...it was hard for her. She wanted the priest to come for the anointing. None of us had the strength to walk to town and fetch him."

I doubt Father Hans would have come. No priest has taken the trail up to the Scharfrichter's home in years, if ever.

"Tomorrow, Marcus. Tomorrow in the morning, would you go find Father Hans? Surely he would not deny last confession, even to us."

I nod. "You should sleep now."

"Not yet. I must say this." She wipes her mouth with a scrap of cloth already stained red. "Should I die in the night—"

I raise my hand against such talk. Elise's hysterics are bad enough.

"Listen to me, Marcus."

Only Tante would I allow to take this tone with me, she who raised me as if her son.

"You should know the truth of your parents. And I am the only one left to tell it."

I stare at her.

"Your mother came to us from Burgau when she was very young, younger even than Sabine. Her parents had lost their crops to blight that year, and had no money. They sold her to your father, for he could find no willing bride."

My father, then. The man who raised me. I should have known, as tall as he was and I taller yet. There was nothing of me in his dark eyes and darker hair that suggested it, but I should have known.

"She was too young, and frail in nature. It was not right that she get with child so early. We were all of us surprised that she lived through your birth. She was so small, and weak. You were not even a month old when she fled with you. It was a cold night, and she in her slippers."

"What happened to her?"

Tante begins to cough again. She does not stop for several minutes. I want to shake her, to exorcise the sickness from her body somehow. But I sit, and wait.

"All was as your father told you. You she left in a basket, covered with a piece of her cloak, at the cemetery gate. It was as far as she could carry you, the poor creature."

The graveyard where I was found lies along the road that curves south and west, toward Burgau. She fled then, returning home and leaving me to whatever future a graveyard could offer.

"We did not know her fate until much later. It snowed heavily the day after they found you, and her body was buried. It was not until spring that one of the gravediggers found her, lying between two headstones. In nothing but her slippers and nightdress."

"Why did he never tell me?"

She shrugs. "He was bitter about it. He warned me against telling you while he lived and then, after he died...I saw no gain in it for you."

"But now?"

Tante sighs heavily. "I do not wish to go to my grave with any secrets. It is bad for the soul."

She rises, not steadily, and wobbles off toward the stairs.

Hund comes and licks my hand. The feel of his rough tongue rouses me from my thoughts.

I get up to look for my shovel.

13

It snows that night. The new snowfall shrouds the grave I dug for Jorg in white. It was no easy task to shovel the frozen ground. The thought of digging more makes my back ache.

Inside the house, on the small landing above the ladder stairs, I listen at the three closed doors. Tante and Gerta sleep in the large room, Elise and Claudia in the smaller. I can hear a pair of rattling breaths behind each door. The air in Jorg's room is silent.

None of the women stirs as I pull on my mask and boots.

The snow is of the heavy, wet sort, and it is hard walking down the hill. The Rabenstein is nearly swallowed by the whiteness. A pair of ravens sit on the scaffold, and caw down a greeting at me as I pass.

Some of the blackened buildings in the Jewish quarter still smolder. And I think the Jews lucky for once. They were burned or driven out before the plague came.

It is too quiet for a market day. Surely not everyone is dead. I see movement in a window of one of the merchants' homes. Someone within is making a cross in black charcoal on the glass. I see a pale hand, a sliver of worried face, and then the curtains close again.

A rat darts across my path and into a pile of straw and refuse near the gutter.

The Marktplatz is empty. Someone has drawn black crosses all along the wall that separates the Rathaus from the rest of town. The Rathaus gates are locked.

But the doors of the church stand open, and as I cross the square toward them—why should I not cross boldly, what worse luck could it bring us all—I see a hooded figure leaving. It is one of the merchants.

As he runs back toward his home, I see him stuffing lumps of something dark into a purse. The priest must be handing out pieces of charcoal, blessed for his flock to use in drawing crosses on their homes.

The merchant's purse is made of fine blue silk, the very same that lies in a bundle in my room, delivered under a layer of eggs at midnight.

Someone is singing inside the church. He has not the voice for so large a space, and the sound is more like wind whistling in a storm than a hymn. The boy stands in the center of the nave. Fever burns in hot red circles on his cheeks.

Father Hans kneels beside him. The priest is anointing a body, its features hidden under a shroud. The dead cover the floor of the nave in orderly rows. Father Hans hurries to finish making the sign of the cross when he sees me approach. The boy notices me, too. He stops singing and scurries away like the rat who crossed my path minutes earlier.

"Scharfrichter, have you not caused enough pain? Leave God's house at once, you who have brought the dying to His children!"

"I have come to ask for a last confession, and anointing."

He laughs, but the sound is hollow and without humor. His eyes are bright with fever. "You've not even been baptized. It would do you no good."

"Not for me. The women in my house wish it for themselves."

He straightens to face me as best he can. His bald head comes up to my chest. "There are good Christians here who seek God's comfort in their time of trial. I have no time to waste on the damned."

He turns from me and moves on to anoint the next corpse. I frown at his back, at the boy singer peeking at me from the shadows of a confessional where he has fled.

I have never read the Bible. But more than one prisoner quoted it in the shadows of the Falterkammer as I went about my work. They begged God for forgiveness, believing it would be given, whatever their crime.

Perhaps the priest is right. Perhaps there is no forgiveness for those of us who live outside the town walls.

I waste no more breath in begging him. The cold walk home will cost me breath enough.

Tante is still asleep when I open her door. She did not wake when Gerta, beside her under the blankets, breathed her last. It is not right for the dead to lie beside the living. I pick Gerta up and carry her to her son's room.

Someone has put Jorg in a shroud. It is an old underskirt of one of the women, carefully split and resewn around him. I wonder if the handiwork was Gerta's last. I set her down alongside him and shut the door.

"Marcus?"

Tante wakes, her voice nothing but a rasp. I sit down beside her on the edge of the bed.

"Marcus, would you fetch the priest for me?"

Her eyes are unfocused already. I have been years among those near death. The Scharfrichter must always be aware of his charge's state, lest he kill him before confession can be extracted and his salary handed over. So I know how close she is to her last breath.

I think for a moment, unsure what to say.

I should give her peace, she who raised me, even if the priest will not.

"Do you not remember, Tante?" I say at last. "He was here but an hour ago. You slept."

"Did he absolve me, and Gerta?"

"Yes."

"Where is Gerta?"

"She is downstairs."

Tante nods. The movement sets off more coughing. She struggles with it, blood spattering out onto her lips and chin. Her eyes tear from the strain.

At last she settles. I ease her back onto the bed and pull up the covers. Only then am I aware that Elise is watching us.

She stands at the door in her nightdress and shawl. Her hair falls in dull yellow tangles around her face. She is haggard. Her beauty is gone.

"You should be in bed." I decide this not only for her sake. I do not like any of them up and around in such a state, watching me with hollow eyes like ghosts.

I shut Tante's door behind myself and take Elise by the elbow. But she shoves off me and totters down the stairs.

I follow her. She is pulling at her hair, her breath somewhere between a wheeze and a sob.

"You do not know," she coughs at me. The blood in her sputum is almost black. "You were not here, so you do not know how it is, in the end. Jorg was in such terror."

She falls against me, and the sound of her crying is like the groan of wagon wheels on a rutted road.

"I am so afraid. Oh, God, how I am afraid." She presses against me. I can feel her hot flesh, only the thin nightshirt between me and her fever. But there is nothing whorish in the way she clings to me. She is a woman terrified, nothing more.

For a long moment, I do nothing but let her lean against me. I do not know what else to do.

And then I know.

"Sit here." I help her into the old rocking chair that Gerta used to draw near the fire. She obeys. There is no fight left in her, only fear.

I choose a trio of vials from the casket of herbs. I take enough from each to make a man my size sleep hard and long. Elise is so much smaller. Then I pour sour cider into the wooden cup and swirl it around. The drink will mask the strong smell of poison.

"This will let you rest for a while."

Elise stares at me. She has watched the whole time. She has no learning in the herbs as I do, but she is not stupid. I see in her eyes she understands.

She grabs the cup and swallows the drink as quickly as she can, lest courage fail her.

"Will it hurt?"

I shake my head. "No. You will sleep."

She nods. Then I offer her my hand. I do not know why; I have never made the gesture before. But she accepts and I help her up. The drink will take effect soon.

On the way to the stairs, she stumbles already. It acts faster than I thought, so large a dose. I pick her up. She feels as light as a child.

"Please, not upstairs. It stinks of death."

I take her to my room, and let her lie on my bed. Already her eyes are closing. The coughing is gone.

I watch her fall asleep. Sleep eases the creases of pain and fear in her face. Her mouth falls open a little. She is beautiful again.

And then she is gone.

I stand there for a long while, waiting. For what, I do not know. I am not glad that she died in my bed, but neither do I wish to move her upstairs. So I stand. Hund comes and stands beside me. Perhaps he does not know what to do either.

At last I go upstairs, but without Elise's body. I will leave it there, in my room. It will be one less to carry down the narrow, steep stairs en route to the graves.

Claudia is dead. Her eyes are open and her body is drawn up as if she died in the midst of a final, painful cough. I draw the blanket over her and close the door.

Tante is dead, too. It is good that she died in her sleep, spared a final agony.

They are all gone. I stand on the narrow landing and think of nothing.

Hund's bark and a pounding on the door rouse me at last. Someone has come.

I put on my mask and open the door.

Ritter Leonhardt does not look so fine and noble as he did on his horse but days earlier, when he and his son hunted rabbits in the forest below my house. He is holding a little girl in his arms. Her pale velvet cloak is stained with a thin line of red that has dribbled from her lips. She looks asleep, but I hear the rattling breath.

"You must save her."

There are shadows under his eyes. His voice is hoarse. I wonder if his coughing has already begun.

"Save her."

I shake my head. "I cannot."

Desperation wells up in his eyes. "You must try. She is my daughter."

I look from him to the child again. I knew as much when I opened the door.

"For the love of God, try, try to help her," he pleads. His lips are slack and rubbery, the words falling out of them without restraint. "She is all I have left. She is my only daughter, an innocent. I can pay. I will give you lands, gold, whatever you ask. Do not turn your back on her, Scharfrichter. It is well known that you know all the witches' brews and potions. Surely there is one that will save her. I would sell my soul for it!"

I shake my head slightly. There is no point in wasting breath on words. I have already told him there is no hope.

"If you had a child, if you had a soul, you would not just stare at her with your dead hangman's eyes! You are worse than the plague!" He shouts this at me. So there is some fight left in him after all.

He does not know of Sabine. None of those who live in the town, below my house and the old lepers' barn and the nightsoil workers' shacks, none of them knows that the tall, slender girl who sometimes visited the Marktplatz was my daughter. They will never know.

"I have graves to dig."

He pales at this. And then he clutches his dying child closer to his chest, backing down the stairs from my door. His thin boots land unsteadily in the snow. But his eyes never falter in their stare. The anger of his outburst is gone. Now there is only fear and grief.

He run-stumbles to his horse and mounts clumsily with the girl in his lap. Their fine velvets and fur-lined cloaks stand out against the snow as I watch them shrink down the hill and back into the town.

I suspect the girl was dead by the time he reined in outside the gate of his home.

I have not finished shoveling the frozen earth, even though the sun long ago set. Now it is cold, bitterly so. The sky above is black, a sliver of moon in it sharp-edged as a sword. I wish for clouds or fog to fill the night sky and absorb some of the wind wailing around me. It whips the edges of my cloak and capuchon like Sabine used to twist and toy with her hair.

Finally I can do no more. I sit on the edge of the pit I have dug and let my legs hang over its edge. I knew better than to try to dig a grave for each of them. The ground is too hard and I am too sore. Instead I enlarged the pit I dug for Jorg. I hope it will fit them all.

It is silent here in the empty night, but for my hard breathing. Pain shoots up and down my legs from the work. My spine feels on fire.

I will have to wait until morning to bury them.

Hund whimpers behind me. He comes up to my shoulder and nuzzles the side of my mask.

I pat his head, but he shies from my touch. Then he circles beside me, as if looking for a spot of comfort but finding none. He moves uncertainly. When he breathes I think I hear a rattling in his lungs.

At last he lies down in the snow, his shaggy wolf head in my lap. I slip off one glove, the cold be damned, and stroke his muzzle.

His mouth is dry, his nose hot. Tears stream from his dark eyes.

I will have to make the grave bigger by one.

I do not heed a warning pop in my back as I lift him gently and carry him, big as he is, back to the house. Inside it is dark and cold. The hearth is gone out. A cloying odor of death wafts down from the bedrooms.

I build a small fire using the last of the kindling and lay him before it.

Then I stretch myself beside him on the cold floor. I stroke his matted fur, and wait for his labored breathing to stop.

14

I dream of the plaguewalker. Again I am running to her down a snowy road. To stop her or to join her I cannot say. I am but a stride behind her when she turns, her red cloak spraying an arc of snow up at me. Her skin is white, lips red and full like her mother's were.

But she has her father's dead eyes.

I sit up in the frigid dawn. Hund's body beside me is cold and the fire in the hearth died hours ago. I wonder if I have been asleep for only one night, or for years. I feel like an old man.

My back and legs complain when I try to lift Hund's body. I lose my balance and fall backward, banging my head against the sharp edge of the bench. The blow stuns me for several seconds. I can do nothing but sit and stare at my dog.

The crack of my skull against the wood smarts. It makes my eyes water and I feel the first trickle of tears down my cheek. They are a surprise.

Like a drunk I rise wobbling and unsteady. I have work to do.

The funeral begins with Elise. Wrapping her body in the blanket from my bed, I drag it out to the pit behind the house. My back explodes in pain with every step.

Once she is in the grave, I use the blanket to bring the others out to her.

It is good that there is no one to see. One man alone cannot both drag the dead out and be at the other end of the blanket to see that their heads do not bang against the stairs or slam into walls. Nor will my sore back tolerate bending down to straighten their limbs after I dump them into the pit.

Hund is last. Perhaps it is wrong to bury an animal with people, but he was a better friend than any I have known. He deserves better than to have his body left for carrion birds to pick over.

I use the last of my strength to cover the grave. Bits of old, dead plants, withered and dark and rotting, mix with the snow and black earth in each shovelful. Ah, I have dug up Tante's garden. It was not much of a plot, just a few rows of onions and some pale flowers she liked to coax into bloom. Gerta would help her, two old women on their knees, fingers caked with dirt, murmuring tenderly to buds reluctant to open in the thin air of our shaded slope.

Sabine would dance around and between them, hair the color of Seidelbast berries twirling all around, like a flower herself, but one with too strong a will to stay rooted. Sabine never helped the women in their gardening. They never asked it of her.

The girl was too spoiled. I ought to have taken more of an interest in seeing she learned the merit of hard work.

I remember then what else grew in the garden. I had a few rows of herbs here that I tended, mostly the purple-flowered Salbei with pale leaves the color of Sabine's eyes as well as my own. I would sell the bitter herb to those hoping to ease the pain of a sore throat or infected tooth. The vain came to me for powdered Salbei, too. They would mix the herb with water and rinse their hair with the concoction to rid themselves of the white flakes that collected on their scalps, as if they forever stood under snow clouds. Arrogant Ritter Leonhardt once came to me just for that purpose.

Most townspeople sought out the Salbei from me for another reason. They say the dead especially appreciate its narrow-petal purple flowers strewn over their resting places.

I throw a final shovelful of dead earth and plant onto the grave. Then it is over. I wonder if I should say something to God, if He is listening. Then I decide against it. No word from me would do them much service.

For a long time I sit beside the cold hearth, at the table where the women made meals and then served them to me. I stare at an old wooden box on a shelf of the open cupboard above the table. For as long as I can remember, Tante would put the day's bread in the box, then lock it until mealtimes, lest Jorg or I claim the fragrant dark loaves for ourselves. The box is unlocked now, and empty. Beside it she has left a precious bag of salt, a half-full sack of spelt, peas, and some turnips and onions. My stomach rumbles.

I pull my boots back on, painful though it is, and then my mask and cloak.

I left my Falterkammer in a bad state, the door wide open, a fire still blazing, a dead man in a heap at its center. It was wrong of me to abandon it, even with the panic that spread through town upon the plague's arrival. Now it is all I have left. I should attend to it.

The way down the Scharfrichter's trail into town is harder than I have ever known. My back tenses with every heavy footfall, and the air is so sharp with cold that I cannot bear to breathe more than a little of it at a time. My eyes tear from the sting of winter air.

As I near the Rabentor, I notice the very stone of the town walls seems paler, as if frozen. Long icicles stretch like demons' fingers from the eaves of wooden stockades built along the tops of the walls.

Once through the gate, I sense a change in the empty streets since yesterday. No wary face peers from a window, no rats crisscross the abandoned alleys. Some of the doors of homes and shops stand open. The air is rife with the acrid, foul stink of burned bodies.

The door of the weavers' guildhall is open, and a pair of legs stretches halfway out, boots in the gutter. The upper half and face of the dead man remain hidden in shadows just beyond the threshold. I wonder if he dropped dead of the plague, or if his demise was sped by looters angry to be disturbed as they pillaged.

"*Mea culpa maxima!*" someone shrieks behind me. I turn and see a woman shuffling toward me. She is naked. The fever burning red on her face must ward off any chill. She is staring past me, toward the Marktplatz and church.

"You! Come back!" another voice, this one male and slurred by drink, shouts from around the corner. Several sets of footsteps crunch through snow that has fallen on streets left unswept.

There are four of them. I know the faces of two. They have spent more than one night in Gilg's charge after brawling. I can guess the others are of their kind.

Petty criminals they are, but dressed like the grandest nobles. They wear fine velvet cloaks and furs, feathered caps tilted crookedly on their heads. The one in the lead, the shouter, wears the heavy gold chain of office that once hung around the Schoeffen's neck.

Their quarry was the woman, but when they see me they stop as one. She totters past, her glazed eyes on the church and imagined deliverance.

The men stare at me.

"It's the damn Scharfrichter!"

"You! The one who brought the dying here!"

"The devil's own henchman!"

I learn too late that the menace of my station has eroded in the terror of the plague. They pounce on me as one animal. Their combined weight topples me.

Four sets of fists slam into me, four pairs of legs find home in my ribs and gut and head. I try to push them off but it is like fighting water.

At last I unsheathe my sword, and swing it above me in wild arcs. The men flee in all directions.

It is several moments before I can stand. When I do, I feel hot pain in my side, my face, one of my knees.

Blood stains the snow where I fell, and most of it is not mine. The sword found home then, more than once.

I hobble toward the Marktplatz. The naked woman is gone. No one else wanders across the square.

Though its brick wall is now blackened with fire, the gates of the Rathaus are still locked. Soot obscures the crosses drawn days earlier. The snow all around the gates is black and trampled down by many boots.

There are no fresh footprints in the snow at the rear door of the Rathaus. Not even looters cared to enter the building through its dank underbelly. The door is unlocked. When I haul it open, a stench hits me as hard as had any of my assailants. I double over and vomit at the stink of rotting flesh.

Then I begin my descent.

I know every measure of space down here. At the bottom landing I feel for the hard edge of a lantern Gilg keeps beside the stairs. I light it with a flint from my pocket and wait for my eyes to adjust to the light.

The fire went out long ago in the Falterkammer. The door is still open, and the smell of old blood and plague leaks from the darkness. I shine the lantern in before entering. All is as I left it.

The pale horseman has begun to rot. What is left of his body is swollen near twice its size, gray-green skin mottled with dark blisters of decay. It stinks worse than anything I have smelled.

I set the lantern on the edge of my worktable and find a clean scrap of bandage to cover my nose and mouth as I work. It does not help much in the close confines.

I ought to carry the dead man out of my room. But I am too sore. I will be rid of him another way.

The hearth in my Falterkammer is small, but I light it anyway and stoke the flames hot as I can. It takes a high heat to burn bone to ashes.

He is of course too big to put on the fire whole. I root around a small closet I have not touched since the man who raised me was killed. My father. I wonder if I should feel something for his memory now that I know the truth of my blood.

I set aside the rusted cat cage, old brands, and screws for thumbs, knees, and toes. The large cleaver I am looking for is near the bottom. Its edge is dull and pitted. But it will do.

I throw him on the fire in pieces, listening to bone and what fat there was on him sizzle and pop. Using the cleaver was harder on my back and bruised ribs than I had thought, and now I can only sit and watch, not without some satisfaction, as the fire consumes him entirely.

The room begins to smell better.

When the last of him is a pile of soot and heat-cracked bones, and I have wrapped my ribs best as I can and smeared mashed Beinwell over my cuts, I let the fire die down. Night has already gathered outside the chamber's high window. It took a long time for the body to burn.

The town outside is as dark as the room in which I sit. Upstairs in the Rathaus, the council is gone. The Schoeffen and his guards, too. There is no one to assign me prisoners who need persuading, or perhaps just killing.

My house, the Scharfrichter's home, is dark and empty. There is no hot supper waiting for me, nor will there be. Hund is not there to greet me. I am to be denied even the women's idle chatter.

The Falterkammer is all I have, and it is of no use without prisoners. So then I have nothing.

I sit there in the dark nothingness, on the hard wooden chair with its restraints dangling off all corners, my legs propped up on the edge of my table to ease the pain in my twisted knee. I sit and wonder what to do.

I must have fallen asleep, bored with my own meandering thoughts, for suddenly it is day outside. Pale creamy light filters in through the window. Not so much that the blades and tongs of my workroom gleam, but enough light to make me stir.

I have been dreaming again. Again the same dream. And now I know why she comes to me as I sleep, red cloak flowing to the ground like an extension of her fire-colored hair, when all else is snow and white as a funeral shroud.

Perhaps I have something left after all. I should go and find it.

I sweep the cobwebs out of the darker corners and straighten all my tools. The cleaner bandages and my healing herbs I pack in an old sack that I used as Loewe to carry unwilling, screeching cats from the alleyways back to the Falterkammer.

When at last I leave my workroom, I lock the door carefully.

The smell of death is stronger out here, in the belly of the Rathaus where Gilg once ruled. I relight my lantern and hold it before me as I enter his half of the prison.

Only five of the cells are occupied, though not with the living. I shine the light in on faces swollen and dark with decay. The last one I see is the Jew. So, he escaped a hanging after all.

Seeing him, his chin that was too narrow for the Kranz now caked with dried blood and sputum, I remember his words. I will live forever, for God does not want me and the Devil is afraid I will overthrow him.

I wonder then why I am the only one in this prison, in this town it seems, untouched by the dying.

Gilg is not in his quarters. He has spent nearly his whole life here, in a single room not unlike a monk's cell, at the end of the prisoners' walkway. His peculiar stink of unwashed, bloated flesh and too much drink is heavy in the air. But it is obvious he never returned here after the pale horseman came. A half-eaten apple and crust of bread marbled now blue and green sit on a wooden trencher on the floor beside his rumpled bedroll. The Schoeffen's guards must have disturbed the big man's breakfast when they dragged the pale horseman and the plague down into his lair.

I wonder if Gilg is dead, or if his fat legs took him fast enough away before the rattle could settle in his lungs.

Up the narrow stairs and into the Rathaus, all here is chaos. What little furniture is left is overturned or singed or both. Court records and pronouncements carpet the floors. Someone has spilled wine, and a good amount of it, over everything.

My boots stick on the purple-stained floors.

The treasury is unattended, its door gone altogether. I shine the lantern inside the room. It is empty, jagged chunks of wood piled on the threshold. Unable to pick the lock of its iron door, the looters chopped away the surrounding frame instead.

I leave by the front door of the Rathaus. Though the gates leading to the Marktplatz are still locked, the looters gained entry by piling refuse on either side of the Rathaus wall in one corner. I climb up the slippery, sooty mountain of old wood and dirt, and then half-fall over the wall to the cobbles of the Marktplatz.

At the last moment I stumble and pitch face-first to the ground. The impact slams my mask back onto my bruised face. I taste blood on my lips.

I sit up and pull off the damn mask. My face pinches from the sudden cold.

I am sitting on the age-worn stones of the Marktplatz, on noon of a market day, bare-faced to all.

There is no one to reprimand me, to fine me, even to shirk back at sight of the face that by law must never be seen.

I look down at the mask in my hands, and it stares back. It is a monstrous creation, no less hideous than the mask my father wore.

I set it beside the Rathaus wall and limp across the center of the Marktplatz. The frozen February air feels good on my face.

15

The house is cold when I enter it. Everything seems colder without my mask. I touch my frozen cheeks and feel the frost that has collected on my whiskers.

And I think of her, alone in the cold for days now, with only her woolen work dress and a cloak. I wonder if she had some money stolen or charmed from the women, or if she at least was clever enough to take some food. Surely she had the sense to take a lantern and flint.

Or perhaps, more her mother's daughter than I figured, she ran off into the night without any thought to provisions.

No, I say to myself. My voice is loud in the empty room. Sabine is spoiled and impudent, yes, but she is not without wits.

I hope I am right.

There is not much in Tante's pantry that will travel well. I do not know how to bake bread, else I would use the last of the spelt and melted snow to make a loaf for the road. The peas and lentils I pour into two small sacks. I recall Tante boiling them for a long time. I take a small pot to use on a campfire.

I am grateful for the turnips and apples. These I know what to do with, and they will keep well.

Then there are the eggs. There are six of them left. I boil them in a pot over the hearth. I do not know how long it will take until they are cooked, so I let them roll and wobble over the fire for most of the evening, until there is little water left.

I crack the shell of one after they cool, for I am hungry enough to eat even an egg. The yolk is gray-green and very tough. So, they are well-cooked.

I eat another, trying to ignore the taste of it. Then I mix the spelt with some snow, until it is a pale brown paste. With some salt it is not so bad. Better than the eggs.

When sunrise comes the next morning, I am already shouldering a pair of large sacks. My back protests at the bundle I have packed of food, some tools, and warm clothes. The heavy wooden coffer will stay behind, though I emptied it of my herbs. Each stoppered vial and bottle I wrapped in a little bit of scrap cloth before arranging them in one of the sacks slung over my shoulder. I took the silk the pregnant maid brought me as payment, too. I do not know why.

It is not easy going, up the hill and past the old lepers' barn. My knee feels hot as I trudge up through snow thick and wet like clotted cream. The clouds above are dark gray and swollen with more snow. They look too heavy, as if they might crash down from the sky under their own weight at any moment, smothering the earth.

I stop just above the lepers' barn, on a naked ridge of ice-crusted rock. I need to rest.

When I look over my shoulder, I can see the whole town. Parts of it smolder. But other than a thin, shifting fog of smoke, there is no movement within the walls. A raven perched on the Rabenstein takes flight just then, and my eyes track it to the bell tower of the church. It sits boldly on one arm of the cross, surveying what is left of Ansberg.

I look nearer my own perch now, down the hill to a cluster of pines that shield the Scharfrichter's home from the worst winds. I can see only part of the steep roof. The rest is hidden from me. Behind the house, the dirt cover of the grave is dark and ugly against the snow.

I have rested long enough.

I turn my back and climb farther up the hill, following by memory the set of boot prints she left. New snow covers them now, of course. In places the drifts come nearly to the top of my boots.

I wonder for a moment how she is faring. Wherever she is, the snow is likely no less deep. And her boots, though big for a girl, are not as tall as mine.

In the afternoon I come to the place where an old landslide wiped out the road. The snow that fell here on the jagged rocks and rubble covered a rippled layer of ice. It is like climbing on greased steel.

I scramble up one side on all fours, favoring my sore knee and sacrificing the other as a result.

The descent is harder. Every few feet I slip, my weight providing momentum for a jarring tumble down rock and ice, until I can grab onto something and stop the fall. Then I start easing my way downward again, until the ice swipes my feet from under me once more.

The flatness of the snow-covered road past the landslide is a relief.

My strides are shortened from their usual length. Climbing that rough mountain of ice and toothy rock was not easy for my battered and sore body. One of my knees has begun to swell. I stop to wrap a large bandage around it. Then I walk again.

At dusk, early now as the fog of thickest winter blankets the land, I stop. The wind is getting colder, and harder. It tugs at the edges of my heavy cloak like a bothersome girl.

I dig in the snow until a patch of naked, frozen earth shows through. Pulling down branches from the skeleton of a nearby tree, I make a small fire. It is not so well-made, for I have never had to camp. Men camp only when they hunt or travel, and I have done neither. The small fire throws off little warmth and shudders in the wind.

The lentils will have to stay in their sack tonight. I cannot figure out how to rig a spit sturdy enough to hold the pot I have brought with me over my poor fire. My first few attempts fail, the branches snapping and collapsing into the flames.

At least it does not snow. I bunch my cloak all around myself, over my head, too, and curl in the snow the way Hund would when he kept me company as I dug graves near the Rabenstein.

Under the heavy wool, it is not so cold. I feel around my sacks. My hands find the rough curve of a turnip and beside it, an apple. I should rub the dirt off them in the snow, but that would mean breaking open the warm cocoon I have made for myself. So I eat them as they are, gritty and tasting of earth.

I will save the hard-cooked eggs for another meal. I am not so hungry as to want them now.

"Ho, there!"

The voice startles me. I sit up and throw off the cloak, dreams of the plaguewalker evaporating in the glint of a morning sun. The dead fire is black at my feet.

A man jumps back from where he stood, not one length from me.

He is older and ruddy in the face, with thick legs and a short trunk. His earth-colored eyes squint at me from under his capuchon.

"You live then." He looks me over. "I thought you were another traveler taken by the cold."

He is holding a jumble of rope and steel and sticks over his shoulder. Two scrawny hares dangle from his belt. His eyes follow mine.

"You've come trapping as well, eh? Don't recognize you."

I stare at him. I am not used to people speaking to me in so easy a tone. Nor does he shy from me, or avert his eyes.

Ah, he expects me to say something to him.

"I am only traveling." My voice sounds as gritty as the turnips that I can still taste in my throat.

He cocks his head at me. "On this stretch of road? Up ahead it's been taken out in a slide, you know."

He glances around, his eyes following my footprints. "But then you know that. Came that way, didn't you? Over the tumble of it, and with all this ice."

He shakes his head at me as if I were a reckless boy. He is waiting for me to say something again.

I stand instead, slowly, to test the knee. It is a little better.

The trapper looks me over again. "Gott im Himmel, you're a tall one. Guess you just stepped over the slide, then, eh?"

He smiles up at me. "Where do you travel?"

"That way." I point to the road ahead. I have never been past the rockslide, and do not know what lies ahead, other than Sabine. Perhaps.

The man was expecting a better reply, I think, for he looks at me as if I were simple.

He takes a step back. "That way, then? I should think so. Not much point in climbing over that tumble on the hill just to camp here a night and turn back, now, is there?"

I look at him for a long time. And I think of two things at once. He may be helpful to me. "I am looking for a girl, tall, with my coloring. Can I have one of the hares?"

"What's that?"

"The hares. You have two. I'm hungry. Can I have one of them?"

The man takes another step back. "For what in return?"

I think of the things I have brought with me. I will not barter my cloak, nor my herbs for poultices and fevers. But...

"I have eggs. Hard-cooked."

"Do you now? How many?" He licks his lips. I am going to have one of those hares. We make the trade quickly, our fingers clumsy in the cold. I suspect he is as tired of eating hare as I am of those damn eggs.

"And this girl you're looking for? What of her?"

I describe Sabine to him, her dress, her features. He thinks for a long time, then shakes his head.

"I've not seen her, though I haven't covered this stretch of forest for several days. Is she a sister, run off or something?"

I shake my head.

The man waits for me to say more, but I am not inclined to do so. There is a long silence. Then he shakes his head at me.

I watch him trudge deeper off the road until his back is gone among the pines.

The hare I tie to my belt. It is cold enough for the meat not to spoil, I think. Ah, I do not know for sure. I should have asked him how long it would keep, or if it need be skinned for cooking. We did not eat hare often in the Scharfrichter's home, and when we did it was bought in market and dressed by Tante.

I stare down at the glazed-eyed animal swinging against my hip and feel my mouth water. No matter. Food is food. I will not go hungry tonight.

16

Perhaps the whole world has died, except for that trapper and me. I walk all that day and see nothing stir from under the snow. I pass no homes, no towns, not even an animal scrabbling back to its den in the cold.

By dusk, when I leave the road to find a place where the wind does not needle me so insistently, I can think of only one thing. The hare will be good in my belly. I ate the rest of my apples at midday, but so much fruit, and raw, too, sits badly in my gut. The hare will take care of that. Chunks of its moist, pale flesh will settle the apples and stop the grumbling my stomach has made for half the afternoon.

This is what I am thinking as I let my bags slip from my shoulder and squat in the snow to build a small pile of twigs and branches. I coax another weak fire out of the wood with my flint, and consider how to cook the carcass that has swung from my belt all day like a hanged man from the gallows.

I find a branch and pierce the hare through with it. Then, holding it over my poor fire, I wait. I do not know how long it will take for the meat to turn a good color, or for the blood to run clear. My gut is impatient, but my arm is strong. I can hold the hare over the fire the whole night if need be.

The juices sizzle as they drip down into the fire. My mouth waters.

A single greedy flame leaps toward the branch and bites it. The brittle wood breaks. My supper falls into the fire.

I rush to save it, using what is left of the branch to drag it from the hungry fire. The branch snaps again.

I shove small mounds of snow onto the fire. The flames are smothered. I am in darkness.

My fingers poke through the debris, feeling warm cinders and snow. Then I find the hare.

Its skin is charred, black in the dim moonlight. But the carcass itself is warm, as if the creature lived again. The flesh is mostly wet and raw.

I am too hungry to care.

My gut wakes me at dawn. What is left of the hare, bones and blackened fur and parts I did not like the feel of as I ate it wolfishly the night before, is strewn between me and the dead fire. I kick a thin layer of snow over it all and gather my things.

It feels colder today, and the clouds sit low and dense just above the trees. It will snow, I think. Then I am glad my back feels in one piece, and my knee is better. Today, I decide, I will keep walking until I find shelter, however many miles that may be.

I do not have to walk far. Before noon, I come to the crest of a treeless hill. Ahead, on the next rise of land, is a small town.

The town has walls, and the familiar high roof of a Rathaus facing a dark-steepled church across a square. But all is on a smaller scale than the town I knew.

As I near, I see the town sits beside a crossroads. Ah, I had not considered that. Sabine would have had three choices for onward travel.

Someone in the town noticed her, surely, as she passed. A girl so fair, long in the leg and with bright hair, would not be missed. Perhaps she has even stayed here.

I am nearly to the shadows of the Haupttor when I realize what has happened.

The town belongs to ghosts now. The main gates are open, unattended. The streets are empty.

The first body I see is sitting along the town wall, just inside the gates. His face is dark and swollen with the first signs of rot. It is a strange contrast to his lank yellow hair. He wears the uniform of a garrison man. The gate guard, likely, maintaining his post till the end.

As I walk up and down the streets, I see that someone lived long enough to overturn carts and shatter the precious glass windows of finer homes. Someone pulled a vast amount of dark velvet curtains into the street from one of those homes, then set the fabric on fire. The charred tatters remind me of the remains of my failed supper. I step over them and continue toward the Marktplatz.

The Rathaus is but a third the size of the one that stood over me as I worked my long hours in the Falterkammer. It is not walled from the town. Its doors stand open, one creaking slightly in a wind that is beginning to pull at my cloak and hair. I turn to the church.

It is old and wooden, though beside it I see someone has broken ground for a proper stone building. A fine layer of frost covers the abandoned site. Nothing will be built there now.

Inside the church, I smell musty, cloying incense that tickles my nose. It does not disguise the stink of death.

I think that most of the town is here. The cold stones of the nave are covered with shrouded bodies, arranged head-to-toe.

The priest is draped over his altar. His head is tilted to one side, a thin line of dried blood from his final bout of coughing streaming unbroken from his mouth down one side of the stone altar. He must have been praying until the moment of his collapse, but for himself or his flock I do not know.

There is nothing in the church for me. I leave it, and walk from building to building, looking for food. I find none. Whoever set fire to the velvet and vandalized the carts was not so deranged that they did not think to empty pantries before they left.

It is past noon now, far enough past that I should think about staying here in the town. There is wood enough to build a proper fire in my choice of home, and to keep myself warm while the snow clouds gathering overhead do their work.

But I do not want to spend a moment more in this place. I do not want to sleep with ghosts.

The sun is already slipping behind heavy clouds when I pass under the Haupttor again and turn my back on the dead town.

I had forgotten about the choice before me, until I am standing in the middle of the crossroads. The roads look the same in all directions, laid out straight across field and low hill as far as I can see.

I mutter into the air, wondering which way Sabine chose. The wind slaps the edges of my cloak against me in response.

Sabine might have changed course here in folly, for she could be a silly girl, laughing at nothing and dancing around our kitchen during meals until I admonished her. Or she might have stayed the course, stubbornly continuing along the same road that brought her here.

She might have turned into town, too. Hers might be one of the bodies rotting forgotten in the church behind me. The thought makes me frown.

I choose the road that is a continuation of the one I have been traveling, and walk into the growing wind.

Snow begins falling near midnight. At least I think it is midnight. I am still walking. There is a weak silver-pink light, from a curve of moon reflecting off snow clouds, that lets me see the road's outline. I do not want to stop, for then I will do nothing but sit and listen to the rumble of my empty gut. So I walk.

It is harder to see once the snow starts. At first it is a white mist. Then it turns heavier, wetter. The shoulders of my cloak are white. The snow cakes under my boots and stings my eyes.

Then the wind decides a new course for the falling snow, and sweeps it all around me in mad circles. I can no longer see the road. I can see nothing at all beyond a swirl of white.

I sink to my knees and pull my cloak around me. Curled in on myself, in the middle of the road, I wait for the snow to stop.

The night is silent but for the angry growl of my stomach.

I throw back my hood and sit up in cold fog. I do not see the slight indentation of the road anymore. Instead there are trees all around me, their branches white as bone with snow. They look like an army of skeletons, arms upraised in protest.

I did not notice the trees last night. I wonder if I missed a turn in the road and wandered into a forest.

A bird flits through the trees to one side of me.

No, it is not a bird. The creature I see has no wings, but wears a cloak the color of blood. She is moving past me, hood drawn up around her face. I cannot see her expression.

I try to stand but stumble on the edge of my own black cloak.

Then I am awake, and the dream is gone.

There are no trees around the place where I fell in the snowstorm the night before. There is only open field and a suggestion of road beneath the snow.

I am still alone then, but for my ever-complaining belly.

I stand well enough, now that I am awake, and brush the snow from my clothes. And then I set off again, down the featureless road that runs arrow-straight to the horizon.

17

It snows again that night. When I open my eyes and feel the weight of snow on my shoulders, the tickle of frost on my beard, I wonder why I did not freeze. Maybe nothing will kill me.

I shake off the snow and feel my limbs snap and pop in protest. I am sore as I have never been, and cold. So cold. The snow snuffed out the meager fire I'd made. A few black twigs stick up from the new whiteness, like limbs of a giant black spider.

The road is only a slight depression in the white expanse of field. I follow it as best I can, stumbling more than once. The snow, newly fallen, is very fine, and as slippery as wadded silk beneath my boots. It is hard going. My legs ache.

I do not think of Sabine, because it does me no good. Either I will find her or I won't.

Instead I think of food. It is foolish, I know, but my mind wanders across the snow, white like fresh milk, like the shells of those hated eggs that now I would devour raw, shell and all. There are some cheeses white as snow. The pale butter Tante used to bring home from market might be mistaken for snow, and so too a boiled breast of chicken, or the heart of a turnip steamed and nicely salted.

I have stopped walking, and am eating snow by the handful. My stomach rumbles angrily in response, cross at me that I should try to trick it into thinking I am eating something. It is hard to start walking again.

The road leaves the fields and curves now through low hills, bubbles in the snow not much taller than I. They remind me of the peaks of sweet clotted cream that Tante would make for Sabine on her birthday.

Ah, there I am, thinking of Sabine again.

I stagger back from an invisible punch. The remains of a hard-packed ball of snow and ice tumble down my chest and land at my feet. It was a good shot, and hit me square in the eye. I wipe away a tear of pain from the impact.

Another snowball strikes me in the chest. Then another. And another.

They come at me like giant hailstones, and some of them as hard. I hold up one hand against the attack and look for its source. I see only white hills.

Another hits me in the mouth. This one was mostly ice, and I can feel the sting of a cut on my lip. The rest of it crumbles into my beard.

"YOU WON'T TAKE HER!!"

My attacker, his arsenal exhausted, leaps up from his hiding place behind a drift. He runs headlong at me like a colt feeling his strength for the first time. I am too cold, too tired, too slow to act before he plows into me. Were I not so big a man, the force of him would have tumbled us both. Instead I only stagger.

He punches me furiously, meaty little fists whamming into my gut, eye-level for him. I am grateful he does not punch lower.

His attack rouses me. I am awake now, for the first time in days.

"You won't! You won't!" He shouts this over and over.

I grab the back of his capuchon and twist it. Then I pick him up like a puppy by the scruff of his neck, and hold him at arm's length. My arm's length. His fists cannot reach me, though he flails and strains. His feet are well above the snow. They kick at me, more than once finding home in my thigh.

I stare at him. He is no more than ten years, maybe less. He is a peasant boy, with a round face and dark, drooping eyes that remind me of Hund's. Someone has cut his hair recently, and badly. He is almost bald, with tufts of uneven lengths sticking out above stubble in random clusters.

At lasts he stops his struggle. Now he is content to glare at me.

"I knew you would come. She told me. But you will not take her."

I draw my brows together, wondering. "Who do you think I am?"

"Death!" He is indignant enough, considering that he thinks Death is holding him high above the ground. "Mama said you were coming, but I will protect her."

"I'm just a man." I set him down.

We look each other over. He looks well fed, and healthy. His clothes are dry. He has not spent the night in the snow.

"Your home is nearby, boy? Have you food for a traveler?"

Suspicion glints in his eye. "You are trying to trick me."

I shake my head and put my finger to my cut lip. I show him the blood. "Death would not bleed, boy. Nor would his empty gut rumble as loud as mine. Your mother, is she sick?"

A look passes over his broad, pale face like a cloud crossing the moon. He shakes his head, but is uncertain.

"If she is sick, I have some medicine with me. It might help. For a warm meal, I will help her."

He looks me over again. No, the woman is not sick. It is something else.

Then he turns and starts walking up a hill, away from the road. I follow.

The cabin is on the crest of another hill, half-hidden by trees. An old barn stands behind it, though I hear no bleating and rustle of livestock. As we draw nearer, I smell old smoke.

Someone built a pyre in the front yard. It is a few days old, and partly covered with snow. Whoever made it did not know the proper way to burn a body. They did not stoke the fire hot enough, or perhaps doused it too early. I can see bones and pieces of a charred shroud poking through the snow.

Beside it, also under last night's snow but newer than the first, is a smaller pyre. It is a campfire, really. As we pass, I see a handful of tiny bones, none longer than my smallest finger.

"Father came home sick from town last market day," the boy says sullenly. He follows my eyes to the second pyre. "My brother. When he died two nights ago, Mama...became as you will see, and it was up to me to give him a funeral. The ground was too cold for burying either of them."

He looks away and wipes his eyes, thinking I do not see. Then he rubs his hands on his trousers. They look too big for him. His shirt drags, catching on his knees. He is wearing his father's clothes.

The cabin before us is poorer than the home of the Scharfrichter was. My father, or perhaps the Scharfrichter before him, could afford finished blocks of stone for the foundation, and sheets of wood specially cut by carpenters in town to join together smoothly. The walls supported a roof steep enough to prevent snow from piling up in winter. He had to build it himself though, or perhaps with the help of some other Scharfrichter he knew. No builders would agree to tramp up the narrow trail past the Rabenstein, no matter what the offered price.

I think the man who built this cabin was no craftsman, either. And he had only the roughest of materials to work with: rocks and rubble, branches fallen or torn from trees. There is no second floor or attic to the cabin, and its thatched roof is rudely crooked against the skyline. Mold lines the edges of chinks between the rocks, some as wide as my finger. One corner of the cabin seems to bulge outward, as if it may divorce itself from the rest of the building at any moment.

The door is made of lashed-together branches over which the builder tacked a layer of thick hide. In places the hide has split apart, and the primitive frame shows through. The boy opens the door hesitantly, then waves me inside.

I must stoop to enter. It is dark. The only light comes from a candle burning low in an old metal holder. It is cold enough that frost huffs out in white clouds with my every breath, and every breath of the boy, who is suddenly breathing faster and harder. He is afraid.

There is no cloud of breath coming from the woman seated at the table, beside the dying candle. The boy's mother for certain, with his same hound eyes and dark hair. She is my age perhaps, or was. Her body slumps to one side in a chair made from wood scraps tied together with old rope. Her eyes are open and unfocused.

I ease myself onto one knee in front of her, tucking two fingers under her jaw joint. There is a pulse, strong but slow.

I lift one of her hands and let it fall back into her lap. Her flesh is warm to my frost-cold fingers, but not as warm as it should be. She gives no reaction.

"Boy, have you any food here?"

He nods and moves into the shadows. I hear him rustling in a bin of what sounds like apples or turnips. My stomach yowls in anticipation.

She blinks. Not so much a blink as a twitch of her eyelids. I stare at her, my face inches from hers. She does not see me.

"Woman, you should rouse yourself, make a warm meal for your guest and your son."

She blinks again, this time thrice and rapidly. Her eyes slowly take me in. If she wonders who I am and what I am doing in her house, she does not show it.

"I am hungry, as is your son. Fix us something to eat."

A tremor passes over her face.

"My son is dead." Her voice is dry, scratchy.

"No, your son is here. Look." I wave the boy over to me. He has been watching me, standing near the edge of the table holding three small turnips. He hesitates.

"Come here, boy."

He comes skulking to me like a dog that has just been hit. Perhaps the woman was cruel to him and beat him. Or perhaps it is something else.

He kneels beside me, earnest eyes on his mother. The woman turns her blank stare on him. I see no recognition in her eyes.

"Do you see, woman? It is your son, left as if orphaned these two days. Rouse yourself to take care of him." And of me, finding some carrots to make a stew with the turnips.

Her hand moves slowly, unsure, to the boy's head. She touches the rough stubble as if it were a saint's relic.

"Brenna, you cut your beautiful hair."

Tears well up in the woman's eyes.

The child lowers her eyes, guilty. "I did not want Death to know me. You said it was coming for us."

The woman is crying now. She clutches her daughter by the shoulder and drags her into her lap.

"God forgive me," the woman weeps, looking at me. "What parent would leave her only living blood to the wolves as I have?"

"She is not so much the worse for it." I look away. The woman has a wild look in her eyes, like that of a prisoner willing to confess to anything. "But surely she is hungry. Have you meat? Bread? Cabbage, perhaps?"

It is Brenna who answers, wriggling her round face out from under her mother's embrace. "The thieves stole most of our stores, but I hid some."

She squirms off the woman's lap and bustles about the house with an authority I would have expected from her mother. I glance at the woman again. She stares at the floor, tears slowing but not ceasing.

"After Papa died, they came in the night," Brenna tells me as she piles more turnips onto the table. "I heard them as they rounded up our goats, and woke Mama so we could hide beneath the bed. They came into the house, and found some of the meat Papa dried—"

"My Friedrich was a trapper, and a hunter," the woman says softly, speaking into the wrinkled collar of her dress. She has the look of a man dropped from the ceiling of the Falterkammer once too often, untethered to anything but pain.

Brenna chatters over her. "They took all our apples, too, our flour and peas, and cherries Mama dried and kept in pretty clay jars. I peeked from under the bed and watched them. They were ugly men."

I nod. It is a lean winter, and there would be brigands on the road even without the chaos that the dying has brought.

"They had daggers and axes," she continues. I wonder if she ever stops to take in breath. Sabine used to chatter like that, endless words as dizzying as watching a pup chase its own tail. "But you wear a sword, so I knew you were not one of them. Are you a knight, then?"

I follow her eyes down my side, to the exposed hilt of my sword of office. I wonder if she notices the skull engraved in the pommel. I shake my head.

"But a soldier, surely. I have seen rich men in town carry a sword, but none with callused hands like yours."

I frown and stand, favoring my sore knee. Brenna glances up as she chops a fat turnip. She is too observant for a little girl, and too curious.

"Mama and I will be glad to travel in the company of a soldier who will protect us from the ugly men," Brenna mutters to her turnips, as if thinking aloud. But she meant for me to hear it.

"I ask only for a warm meal, and then will be on my way."

"Where does a soldier travel, alone and without a horse, in winter?"

"I am looking for my daughter." I do not know why I answer this little girl as if she merited hearing my story. Perhaps it is because it is good to talk to someone other than myself, someone alive and not staring at me from a dream.

She cocks her head like a dog that has heard a curious noise.

Her interest may have some value, I realize. From her little armory of snowballs she could see far along the road.

"Perhaps you have seen her pass by. A tall girl, with hair and eyes my color and a very fair face. She may have traveled the road six or so days ago."

Brenna frowns down at the turnip. "We have seen no one but the thieves in that time. But if we come with you, we can help you look for her."

"I need no help."

"But you have not found her yet, looking on your own."

She bites her lip at my glare and hunches over her turnips, chopping them all the faster.

I glance at the woman again. She is breathing more normally now, though her eyes dart all around the room as if she is tracking ghosts. Or demons. Her gaze comes to rest on me for a long moment.

"We will die with no food," she whispers. I hear resignation in her voice.

Brenna's knife slams down on the table, harder than need be through a wilted head of cabbage. She is scowling at her mother.

"It is a hard winter for traveling. You would do better to stay here than join me." It is true enough, as true as it is that I do not want to be slowed by a wild-eyed woman and her snowball-throwing daughter.

"We will die here." The woman nods to herself.

"I shot a hare this morning," Brenna announces brightly, looking for praise on our faces.

She lifts the cloth that covers a pot near the door. The pot is full of half-melted snow, but I see chunks of skinned meat peeking through. I raise my eyebrows as much in surprise as in anticipation.

Brenna sees her new value. "Papa taught me to hunt, to help him when he needed an extra hand. I have a good eye, and small fingers to rig the trap knots very finely. I can help you hunt when we travel."

"I do not hunt."

The woman is watching me closely. For a moment her eyes glimmer with thought. But she says nothing.

"What do you do for food?" Brenna asks, eyes wide with disbelief.

"I buy it at market." It is near enough the truth. They do not need to know I am a Scharfrichter.

I look Brenna over again. She is a sturdy young thing, not the spoiled sort given to complaining, I'd guess. If the girl can hunt, travel may not be so lean. I glance back at her mother. She stares at my sword. Now, with her eyes still and averted, I notice she is not ugly, nor even as plain as I first thought. She has strong peasant hands, too. She could carry some of my things, and lighten the load on my back and sore knee.

Brenna lights the hearth and sets the pot of vegetables and hare over it. My mouth waters. It would be good to have meat as I travel.

"What say you, woman? You and your daughter will travel with me?"

"Death is coming," she says, staring at my boots.

"Maybe so. But come with me and you'll be safe enough. I walk ahead of Death."

Her dark eyes meet mine. "Yes, I think you do."

18

It is the best stew I have ever had.

It has no taste, and lumps of fat float on its gray surface, but I cannot eat it fast enough. The vegetables have been overcooked to a dark mush that sinks to the bottom of my wooden bowl as soon as Brenna ladles it from the pot. The chunks of meat are tough as the thick strips of leather I sometimes used to gag prisoners who screamed too much. But I do not care, and neither does my grateful belly. I nod my approval as Brenna sits down before her own bowl.

The woman does not eat. She stares at the stew as if expecting it to attack her at any moment.

"Have you any bread?" I ask Brenna.

She shakes her head without looking up as she drinks directly from her bowl.

To compensate for the lack of bread, I help myself to another bowl. At last my stomach quiets.

"Mama, you should eat."

The woman makes no move to do so.

"It will be hard travel on the winter roads," I say, pushing her bowl toward her. I do not want her slowing me down. "You will need your strength."

Her face trembles like that of a man entering the Falterkammer for the first time, sure that nothing good is in store.

All at once she flings the bowl away, into the hearth.

"Mama!" Brenna shouts as she jumps up and runs to save the wooden bowl from the flames.

The woman can move quick enough, after all. Before her daughter, she is at the hearth, reaching into the fire for the bowl.

She does not shriek when the flames bite her flesh.

I am behind the woman then, dragging her back from the hearth. Yanking up the folds of her skirt, I wrap them quickly around her hand to smother the fingers of flame on her cuff.

The air is sharp with the smell of burned wool. Brenna dodges from one side of me to the next, trying to see the damage done, as I ease the woman down into her chair.

She stares absently at her burned hand, as if it is of no particular concern to her. When I pull aside the wad of skirts around the burn, she does not even flinch.

The cuff of her sleeve is black and singed. Several rows of bead-like blisters rise on the back of her hand, and the whole of it is red and swollen. But she is fortunate. The burn is not so bad. I suspect it is painful more than anything else, though she does not show it.

I hear what sounds like Hund behind me. Brenna is growling, her face as red as the burns on her mother's hand. Her eyes are black with anger at the woman.

"Fetch me some snow, girl, and be quick about it."

She blinks at me, then nods and races out into the night.

"Brenna was wrong to serve me using Friedrich's bowl," the woman says stiffly. I ignore her, turning her wounded hand over to see if the palm was burned as well. It was, and two of the fingers blister worse than the rest. All this, over a dead man's bowl.

When Brenna returns, holding the hem of her father's shirt out before her, piled with snow, I tell her to pack the woman's hand in it. I look through my supply of herbs for a small vial of oil infused with Johanniskraut.

The blood color of the oil makes the woman's burns look worse. I dab it on carefully, so as not to break the blisters. The oil I made last summer. It was one of the few times Sabine was useful to me. She sat at my side as I steeped the yellow Johanniskraut flowers in a shallow pan of nut oil, patiently separating the flowers petal by petal from their stems, careful not to tear or crush the fragile blooms. She was trying to charm money off me for some sweets, I recall. I think I did give her a coin for her good work, but I do not remember for sure.

Brenna watches me as I wrap the woman's hand with a long scrap of bandage. The anger brews behind her eyes still, and she bites her lip to keep from shouting out at her mother.

"Have you another bowl?" I ask, tying off the bandage without looking. I have done it often enough.

She nods.

"Then fetch it for your mother. She has not had her supper yet."

Both of them knit their brows. Brenna obeys, but I can tell she would like just as well to let the woman go hungry. If she can still feel hunger.

I take the filled bowl from Brenna and set it before the woman.

"I will not be slowed by a woman swooning from lack of food. Eat the stew or I will pour it down your throat myself."

Her eyes flick over me. She says nothing, but takes up her spoon reluctantly. She eats like an old woman, slowly, her hand unsteady.

Brenna busies herself cleaning up the puddle of spilled stew from the woman's first bowl. She glances up every now and then, to make sure the woman is eating. I can guess from the tightness of her young face that this is not the first time her mother has lost her wits.

At last, her temper calming as the woman's bowl empties, Brenna sits back down at the table to attend to her own supper. She starts to chatter again. She wants to know everything. Where are we going? When will we leave? I do not know the answers to many of her questions.

She ladles the last of the stew into my bowl, smiling a little. She is proud to have cooked this meal, and happy because she sees her value to me.

She sits and watches me as I eat, her chin resting on her hands and eyes upturned like a dog begging for scraps. Sabine would do that, usually when she wanted something.

I wonder if all little girls are so cunning, or if I have encountered two of the more devious of their kind.

"We will leave in the morning," I tell her.

She nods as if I were a priest at the pulpit. "I will gather all the food that is left, and Papa's traps and tools."

I nod back at her. She lists for me all that the thieves left behind, and I tell her what to pack, what may be of use to us on the road. It is the nearest to a conversation that I have had in months, I think.

I do not address the woman. There is no point. She sits staring at her empty bowl, thoughts elsewhere.

“We cannot leave them,” she says suddenly. Her cheeks flush at the abruptness of her own voice.

“Who?”

“My son. And my Friedrich. We must find hallowed ground for them. We cannot leave them to the wolves.”

Brenna glances sidelong at me, anxious.

“They are at rest now, woman, let them be—”

“No.” She glares at me. Her jaw tightens. Maybe there is some spirit left in her after all. “I will not leave their bones to be gnawed by animals. We will take them with us.”

I could leave the two of them here, with their ghosts, but then I would not have someone to hunt for me. A thought crosses my mind.

I stand and rummage through my things again. My rough hands brush against the blue silk I keep folded in the same sack as my herbs.

“Do you see this?” I hold up a dark metal flask stoppered with cork. Within it is a clear spirit that I keep on hand to stave off fits of coughing and chills. I shake the flask so that she can hear the liquid slosh around inside.

She nods, unsure.

“It is holy water, from the church of my town,” I say, setting it on the table carefully. “If I consecrate ground with it, and then bury your man and son, will you be satisfied?”

“The ground is too cold—” Brenna presses her lips together when I glare at her.

The woman thinks this over. Her eyes study the flask. She nods again.

I slip the spirit into a pocket of my trousers and tell Brenna to find me a shovel.

The girl follows me out into the dusk. She walks only half a step behind my heels, as Hund used to do when still a puppy, before he learned it was no pleasure to feel my boot crash down onto his paws. I elbow her back when her eager little feet nearly trip me.

She runs alongside me, tucking her hand into my belt.

“Be off, girl. Go back to your mother.”

I glance over my shoulder. Soon it will be too dark to see much from the half-open door of the trapper’s home. That is good, for my purposes.

"What are you going to do?" Her teeth chatter, as much from nervousness as cold, I think.

I do not answer. It is better if she does not know.

"Papa was a very good man," she says quickly. I hear apology in her voice. "He loved Mama very much, and was very kind. It is hard for her, without him."

"Go inside, girl. Busy your mother with packing. Keep her from looking out at me."

I hear her footsteps crunch in the snow, back toward the cabin.

Then I am beside the pyres. It was a job poorly done, and as I brush away the new snow with the back of my borrowed shovel, I can see that most of both bodies remain. I glance back toward the cabin, but there is no curious face at the door.

I trace a grave-sized rectangle in the snow nearby, scraping off the white until brown dead grass and black earth show. I test the soil with my shovel. The first few inches are not frozen through. It will be enough.

By now it is dark. There is just enough moonlight, glinting off the snow, for me to see what I am doing. I dig all the soft dirt out of the grave, and pile it carefully to one side. Then I use the shovel like a broom, sweeping what is left of the woman's husband and son into the center of the shallow hole.

At last I arrange the dirt over the bodies in a little mound. I have dug enough graves to know what they should look like. It is a neat illusion. The first heavy rains of spring will loose the bones from the dirt if curious animals do not do it sooner, but we will be long gone.

I wait for a long time in the cold, after I am finished. I do not want to return to the woman too quickly, lest she guess what I have done. The work has warmed me well enough against the cold, anyway. Only when the sweat along my spine and arms begins to chill do I turn back to the cabin.

"It is done, then?" The woman is standing, her back to the door. Orange light from the hearth silhouettes her rounded frame. She is not so small as she appeared at first, slumped in the chair. She has been arranging a pile of warm blankets before the fire.

I nod.

She turns partway to me, and I see something shy, apologetic almost, in her manner. It is an improvement over her earlier mood. "It must have been hard work, in the cold. I cooked the last of the cabbage for you, with some apples."

There is a bowl of food on the table. Inviting little curls of steam rise from it, beckoning me.

She is a better cook than her daughter, I think. Brenna is already asleep on the bed in one corner. The woman glances from the girl to me, considering something.

"It will be warm for you, before the fire," she says quietly, gesturing to the bedding she has laid out for me. She does not wait for my answer, but turns her back and climbs beneath the covers, beside her daughter.

I listen to their light breathing as I unfasten my boots. Perhaps it will be good to have them with me as I travel. The girl is capable enough, and I think the woman will be too, once she is recovered from her grief and has her wits about her once more.

Then I wonder, as I slip between two thick blankets warmed from the heat of the fire, what it must be like to grieve as she does for someone so loved. I would not know.

19

When dawn comes, I am in no hurry to stir from my makeshift bed before the hearth.

It is warm, the blankets are soft. Even the smell of the woman and her girl is a comfort, reminding me of home. They are still asleep, one breath light and slow, the other restless.

I listen for a while. It is the woman who sucks in her breath like a man poorly hanged. I think even in her dreams she chases ghosts around her home.

Last night she was different, though. For a moment then, when she stood silhouetted by the fire, there was something of interest in her face as she watched me come through the door. Perhaps she is warming to me. She did not need to cook those apples for me last night, when I suspect she and the girl went to bed with empty stomachs.

I consider this for a while, before drifting back to sleep.

A clattering of pots wakes me. The woman is standing beside me, tending a pot over the hearth. Her skirts rustle in my face. The cabin is warm enough that she need not wear her heavy woolen leggings indoors, and for a moment I glimpse her bare ankles. They have a fine curve to them that reminds me of Elise.

Brenna sits at my feet. "Who is Sabine?"

She might as well have thrown snow on my face. I sit up, wide awake, and forget about a dead woman's feet. Instead I remember how I came to be at this cabin, in the middle of nowhere.

"My daughter."

"You were talking to her in your sleep just now."

Brenna glances up at her mother's back. The woman is silent.

"And what did I say?" I did not know I spoke in my sleep. I wonder if I always have.

"That she should stop walking so fast. That she ought to wait for you."

I rub my eyes. The strength of the light leaking through chinks in the walls tells me it is a few hours past dawn. We should hurry, or risk falling another day behind her.

I pull on my boots and roll up the blankets. They will travel well with us.

The woman hands me a bowl full of gray liquid. I think I smell barley in it, but it is mostly water. Her hand does not move away when I take the bowl. It is not the hand that she burned yesterday, but I notice it is bandaged as well. An older scrap of cloth is wrapped around the wrist, and clumsily tied. Not my handiwork for certain. A thin line of blood soaked through long ago from whatever wound is beneath the wrap.

She and Brenna notice at the same moment that I am looking at the bandage. Brenna looks at the floor in shame and frustration. The woman slips her hand away.

"You are a good father, to search so hard for your daughter, even in your sleep." There is some other thought behind the woman's words, but I cannot name it.

I must be a bad father, to let her run off in the first place. I scald my lips and tongue in a rush to drink the hot liquid. "We should leave soon, to have good light when we travel."

They gather their belongings as I sip the filmy porridge. Then the woman douses the fire in the hearth. She takes a look around, at her home. Her eyes are wild again, and for a moment I think she will protest leaving.

She looks at Brenna, and then at me. She is thinking again.

Brenna is the first through the door. She wears a trapper's pack half as tall as she is. To it she has tied a blanket roll, an assortment of traps, her bow, and a packed quiver of arrows. She turns clumsily with the burden to see what is taking us so long. For her this is an adventure.

For her mother, lingering just inside the threshold, it is the end of all she has known. Her eyes run over every corner and crevice.

"Come now, woman. There is nothing left for you here."

She looks at me again with a hunted expression, and steps out into the weak sunlight.

Outside I see that something has disturbed the hasty grave. She sees it at the same moment, and stops to look.

The neat mound I left was knocked over in part, then repiled. It must have been Brenna who did this, earlier in the morning. She added a crude cross made of lashed-together branches to the center of the mound.

The girl looks at me, anxious. She knows then. I can guess she saw how shallow their resting place was. She fixed it well enough, though, and I see no evidence that will tell the woman what I have done.

Her mother kneels at the foot of the grave, staring at the cross. Brenna and I look at each other. We are nervous, standing behind the woman like children who have misbehaved and fear being found out.

"I go easier, knowing they are on hallowed ground."

The woman stands again, shouldering the bundle of food. Her eyes are dry but empty.

She does not look back.

My progress is slower with them. I am partly to blame, for I insisted on taking all the bedding they had, better to keep us warm. I carry half of it on my own back, which does not care for the added weight. Brenna gave me her father's old pack, but his shoulders were narrow. The wood frame hits me wrong, and its leather straps chafe. The wide belt meant to buckle around the dead man's waist squeezes my ribs when fastened.

"How far is the town?" I ask Brenna, who leads our procession.

"It is behind us." Her mother answers. So, her Friedrich brought the plague from the ghost town I passed a few days earlier. I am suddenly glad to hear it. Perhaps the next town will not have been emptied already by the dying.

"What lies ahead?"

"Wuerzberg, but not for several days' travel."

I frown. We do not have food to last more than two or three days.

We do not get far that day. When the wind rises and the sky loses its color, I do not push farther. They are both tired, as am I.

We camp in a small clearing a little way off the road, surrounded by tall pines. It is good shelter from the wind.

Brenna builds the fire. It is a task she knows well. I watch her as she tips branches in on each other to form what looks like the roof of a very small hut. The flames burn bright and strong.

The woman says nothing, sitting with her knees drawn to her chest and eyes staring into the fire. She is thinking again. It bothers me that a woman could think so much and say so little. I am not used to it.

After we eat, Brenna curls in on herself like a dog beside the fire. I wonder that her mother does not notice the girl lying so close to the flames. An errant spark could set her clothes on fire. But the woman is absorbed in thought. She stares at the flames. And then at me.

"Why do you look at me like that?" I am used to so intent an expression only from prisoners in the Falterkammer.

"You have eyes the color of my Friedrich's," she says quietly. There is something in her voice, in her dark eyes, that reminds me of the ravens that perch atop the Rabenstein. "Though his sparkled with life, until the end. Then they turned flat and cold, like yours."

I say nothing.

"Scharfrichter."

She says the word again, accusingly.

I nod. What does it matter to her, anyway? Were it not for me, she would have frozen to death in her own home by now, and her child with her. I lean back onto my pack, behind me in the snow, and tuck the blankets in around myself.

"I knew by your manner, by your sword. By your dead eyes."

She is weeping now. Tears stream down her face like a river thawed all at once. Brenna stirs and rolls away from us and the fire, but does not wake. I suspect she is used to the sound of her mother's tears.

"God forgive me that I could not care for my own daughter, that the task would fall to a Scharfrichter. I do not deserve Brenna."

I give her my back. I had enough of sobbing fits when Elise lived.

After a time she quiets, which is good. I am tired and need to sleep.

"Our town had no Scharfrichter," she says lowly, just as I shut my eyes. "It was too small for one, or too poor. Or its people law-abiding enough."

I pull the top blanket over my ear. I do not care to hear about what the town behind us was like. It is gone now, as completely as if God swept it off the earth.

I hear a rustling at my back a heartbeat before her ragged breath stirs the air. I open my eyes to find her close beside me, staring.

"But I have heard tales." She nods to herself, rocking to and fro like a man whose mind has been broken along with his legs in the Falterkammer. "Is it true the Scharfrichter can offer to marry a condemned woman, and that if she agrees her sentence is revoked?"

I nod. The law exists, though I never had the desire to invoke it. The last thing I needed was the chatter and moods of another woman in my house.

"They say most women prefer to go to their deaths, rather than wed Death's henchman."

I nod again. I have heard it so.

"Was your wife one of the condemned?"

I frown at her over my shoulder. "I never had a wife."

"But, you've a daughter..." She is rocking faster as she squints and scowls at me.

"One of the whores birthed her."

She stops her bobbing. Her eyes no longer dart around my blankets, the fire, the stars overhead. Now they are fixed on me like those of a falcon on its prey. Suddenly I am uneasy. There is too much thought behind those black eyes.

"Is it so, then?" she asks in a whisper. "Only whores and condemned women would traffic with a Scharfrichter?"

I roll away from her again, though now I am full awake. I do not like the idea of sleeping with that woman at my back. Sooner would I sleep with wolves.

"Which am I, Scharfrichter?"

I start. Her whisper is against my ear.

"Leave me be, woman."

But she is rambling now, her voice low and hot against my cheek.

"I who let my husband and son die, and would have led my daughter to a shallow grave beside them were it not for Death's own henchman come to us. My Friedrich is in heaven now, shedding tears that I can find no better company than Death itself. Or he is in hell, because I could not bear to leave him to call for the Father for anointing—"

"Hush, woman!" I sit up and shove her back to her own bundle of bedding.

"—even that is just as well, for I know my sentence cannot be commuted. I am damned. I have failed as wife and mother, and the task of caring for my blood would fall to you—"

I lean toward her and clamp my hand over her mouth. She does not fight it.

"Quiet yourself, woman, else you anger a tired man more!"

I feel her teeth on my palm. She bites into one of the callused pads, not in attack, but something else. I take my hand away. It leaves a red blotch on her sallow skin.

She grabs my hand and pulls it back to her mouth. Her raven eyes stare hungrily at me.

"What is it, woman?"

She is on me all at once, straddling me, hiking up her skirts. Her fleshy thighs dimple from the cold.

"What are you doing?" I demand as her hands fumble under my cloak.

"Whores and the condemned—" Her whisper is more of a growl.

Her fingers are like icicles on my belly. I am too surprised to shove her aside.

"I am already one, why not the other." Her lips slam against mine as if in anger. She is not skilled like Elise, nor docile like Claudia. It is more like handling a wild animal that has been cornered.

But I do not push her off me. Her touch, almost violent as it is, is not unwelcome. She is alive, and I have been too long among the dead.

I try to roll over onto her, but she has me pinned, her strong peasant legs clamping my bruised ribs as tightly as the Boot on a prisoner's legs. There is such wildness and rage to her. For a moment I imagine she does not intend to lie with me, but to devour me and leave only a pile of gnawed bones behind.

She makes no sound as we move as one beneath the blankets. Her mouth, it seems, is only for biting. I feel her teeth on my ears, my neck, the whiskers of my beard.

Even when she arches suddenly, and I feel her body shudder along with mine, her mouth remains ungentle.

She bites my lip, still swollen from her daughter's iceball, hard enough to split the fragile scab. I wince with the sudden pain and turn my head from her attack.

"The dead bleed," she murmurs, her own lips smeared red.

"I am not dead, woman."

She leans onto my chest with the weight of a corpse. Her fingers trace with sudden tenderness down my nose, along my jaw, around my brow.

"Eyes so like his," she says in a lover's whisper. But the words are not meant for me. "No, you are not the dead one."

For a moment we lie there as if the winter winds have frozen us so. Then her lips meet mine again.

It is different this time. The animal has been caged. There is a softness to her kiss. I do not need to see her face to know she is crying.

And I wonder if this is how she touched her husband, the trapper with eyes my color lying with his son behind us in the snow.

She pulls my blanket up until it nearly covers our heads. Her warmth and touch are welcome, even when her fingers trace the scratches she gave me on my shoulders and chest, the flesh swollen and tender.

At last she rolls off me, stretching herself along my side with her back to me. My heavy breath is the only sound other than the crackling of flames. It is as if she does not breathe.

I stare at the faint outline of her shoulder, and the dark tangle of hair tumbling down it and onto my chest. She stirs when I touch her, and inches away. My side feels a cold draft.

Her eyes are open. I can sense it. And she is thinking. Of what, I can guess. It may be my body beside hers, but in her mind it is her Friedrich. Or perhaps she is rambling to herself, thoughts pacing up and down the dark halls of her grief-addled mind.

I turn my back to her at last. Let her dream of ghosts, if she wishes. Perhaps as the miles grow between her and the poor grave behind us, she will not find the company of a Scharfrichter so terrible.

I do not dream of the plaguewalker that night. I wake at dawn. Brenna and I are alone beside a dead fire. The woman's footprints lead off into the forest that circles our camp. To relieve herself, likely.

Brenna is still asleep, her cloak and a patched gray blanket drawn over her head and tucked in on all sides. When my stomach rumbles, I think of waking her to fix me breakfast. Then I decide against it. Her mother will do a better job.

When I stand I feel new soreness where the woman scratched me like a starved cat. The wounds sting in the cold air, even under my shirt. I straighten my clothes and set off to find her.

Her footprints are easy enough to follow. They weave through the cluster of pines that shielded our little camp, and then into a spinney of lesser trees, their leaves shed and limbs naked in winter's cold.

I am not twenty steps when I see where the footprints end.

She walked a short way in the forest, just far enough to be out of hearing.

I run the last fifty feet, my eyes on the pale piece of fabric. It is her underskirt. Rolled and hung from a thick branch only inches above my head, it made a strong noose.

She must have climbed out onto the branch and knotted the skirt around the tree, then her own neck.

She dangles now from the tree, swaying a little. The branch above her creaks. The woman's face, dark from the excess of blood trapped in her head, is level with mine. Her eyes are open. Her mouth is open as well, lips blue and swollen. She has been dead for hours.

"Mama?" Brenna's voice is shrill like a raven calling. I hear her feet crunching through the snow toward me. She stops a few paces away.

"Mama?"

I look at the girl. Her eyes are dry, but her features are very pale. She stares at me, awaiting explanation. I have none to give.

20

Of course I cannot bury her. Even if the ground were not frozen, I have no shovel. I think of burning her. It seems indecent just to leave her here, now that I have cut her down and loosed the fabric that choked life from her.

Brenna kneels beside her, arranging her mother's thick hair. She pulls it across the woman's neck to hide the mottled flesh. The tresses spill onto the snow, the blue-black color of carrion birds stark against the white.

"Mama does not want to be burned," Brenna says, looking up at me. She has such serious eyes for a child.

I nod. I will do as the child wishes. The woman was her mother after all.

"We will bury her in the snow, with blankets, so that she stays warm until the angels come for her."

I nod again and watch as she sits back on her heels and begins sweeping snow onto the woman. There would be no gain in telling her that the woman is beyond warmth, or that wolves will likely come within the hour to snuff aside the snow in search of food. Nor do I stop her from draping one of the blankets we brought with us over the mound. We will have to leave more than that behind us, now that there is one less in our party to shoulder a pack.

"What will we do now?" she asks, brushing the snow off her father's baggy trousers. I am surprised that she does not cry. Instead she stands facing me, hands on her hips.

"We walk."

We take up our packs and turn back to the road. But part of me still stands beside that tree, looking eye to eye with the dead woman. Her intent was plain in her words last night, I understand now. And I should never have mistaken her touch as meant for me. She was making love to a ghost, and to the death she desired.

I plow through the snow, angry then. With every step the straps of the ill-fitting pack rub against my scratched shoulders, reminding me at once of the woman and her beloved, narrow-shouldered Friedrich. My mood darkens.

"Please!" The voice is far away, like the squawk of a bird high overhead. I look over my shoulder and see Brenna is a good way behind me. "I can't walk so fast!"

I am not walking fast at all. Then I remember my legs are nearly as long as she is tall.

She comes running at me like a puppy that has not learned to use all its paws at once. Her face is red as blood.

"Please! Slower!"

I nod and start walking again. My stomach grumbles. It sounds like wolves. We will finish the turnips and apples tonight. And what next, I do not know.

"Please!" Her voice is far behind me again.

This time as she runs to me she falls, sprawling face down in the snow. When she struggles to her feet, I see her cheek is bleeding. Caught on a stone or half-buried twig, likely. Tears well up in her eyes over the pain.

"Please, you must not walk so fast!" She sucks in air as if she is drowning. And then I see the tears are not for the cut on her face. "Please, do not leave me here! Please, don't! I do not want to be alone!"

She bawls like a newborn denied its mother's breast. I stare at her and wonder if she will ever stop. Then I remember I lost a cook and a bedwarmer this morning. But Brenna lost more.

"I will walk slow for you."

She is embarrassed now over the tears, and wipes them off roughly like the little boy she pretends to be. We fall into step with each other.

The road here is straight, over flat land, and good for travel but for the snow. In places it has fallen so deep that I step into it nearly to my boot top. I glance over to see how she manages.

Her face is a brilliant red, brighter even than before. She is breathing like a wounded animal, all ragged and in panic.

She looks at me anxiously, worried that she is going too slow to suit me.

I stop. She doubles over, hugging her knees and wheezing. Her pack slips forward and over her shoulders, tipping her headfirst into a snowdrift.

It is not fair for either of us. I should not have to walk so slow that I cannot maintain momentum, and each step is as if the first. And the snow that tops my boot comes nearly to her waist.

I pull her up and refasten the pack around her soft shoulders. Then I take off my own bundle and set it on the snow. It is simple enough to flatten the roll of blankets tied to the top, making a seat.

I hoist the pack back onto my shoulders.

"Here, stand behind me." I kneel on one leg. "Climb up so you sit on the pack, and your legs are around my shoulders."

She obeys. Then I hold on to her legs to steady the both of us.

She gasps when I stand. I imagine the world looks strange when one is suddenly twice as tall.

It is not easy going through the snow with her on my back, but only because of balance. She is light enough. I have hauled men four times her weight to and from the Falterkammer, to and from the Rabenstein. Only when she shifts and I am mid-step is it difficult.

We tumble suddenly into the snow. She flips over me as I fall onto my knees. A buried branch tripped me.

I sit back on my heels and rub my shoulder. Her boot found home in it as we fell.

She is lying on her belly, head raised and staring into the forest at the edge of the road.

"Are you hurt, girl—"

"Shhhhh." She holds up her finger at me like a woman admonishing her child. "Do you see it?"

I look in the direction that has caught her attention. I see dark pines, branches slung low under the weight of snow.

Then there is movement at the base of one of the pines. It is a hare. Why it is not sleeping in its warren, I cannot imagine. This is no weather for such a creature to be about.

Brenna wriggles out of her pack. She unties her bow from the pack's frame and crawls away from me. And I am surprised to see her soft child's body slither over the snow. It is so quiet I can hear my own heart beating in my ears.

My stomach thunders then. She scowls over her shoulder at me before continuing her advance.

She is halfway to the hare, who sits shivering beneath the tree. I wonder if it is ill. It is scrawny enough.

I hear a soft twang as Brenna looses the arrow. It hits the hare neatly in the side. The animal twitches once and slumps over on its side.

Brenna runs to it, clapping her hands. She is a little girl again.

We build a small fire near where she killed the hare. I watch as she skins the kill with the precision of a man thrice her age. My gut rumbles in anticipation. Suddenly I am very glad I did not leave her beside her dead mother.

She makes a spit for the fire using branches torn from the trees. Then the two of us crouch in the snow, watching the meat cook.

It was indeed a scrawny hare, and its meat is stringy. With it we eat the last of the turnips, roasted in the fire until their skins blistered black.

The light is fading when we finish. I can see far enough ahead on the road to know we will not find shelter this night. It is best to sleep now, when our bellies are full.

"We'll rest here." I crawl under the nearest tree. It is shelter enough from a light but frigid wind, and the snow is not so deep here.

Brenna sits beside our fire, watching me. She pokes at the hare's bones with a twig. Her eyes are large and fixed. Again I think of Hund as he sat beside the table, waiting for scraps from my plate.

I turn away from her and curl up against the rough bark of the tree. Still her eyes stick into me like heated pokers. Ah, if she wants or needs something, let her ask. It is not my manner to inquire after the whims of little girls.

She creeps over to me as if I am the next hare to be felled by her bow. I open one eye when I feel her beside me.

She slips the edge of my cloak out from where I tucked it, along my thigh, and wraps it around herself. She is a brazen creature, to be stealing a man's cloak.

And then she snuggles along my back, burying her hands into the folds of my clothing. I feel her stubby fingers along my spine.

She is warm enough for so small a creature. I do not mind her there. But I worry I will roll over her in my sleep, smothering her. And then I would have no meat as I traveled.

I turn and put one arm around her. She presses her shorn head into my chest. And then she is asleep. I am soon to follow.

It is near noon when we wake. I was more tired than I realized from the travel. For a moment I am angry to have slept so long, for I am not a man given to loitering. But then I am glad to wake with the sun already high above me. Better that than open my eyes again to the purple and gray gloom of a dying night.

It is a weak winter sun, the color of butter, and very small in the sky above us. I crawl out from under the tree to sit in the light, and let the side of my dagger catch its rays and throw them back up into the cold air as I sharpen the blade.

Brenna wakes at the scrape-scrape-scrape of blade against my cheek. She comes to sit beside me, eyes wide. At first I think she is staring at the palm-sized piece of polished metal I have balanced on one knee.

I ignore her, my eyes on my own reflection in the metal as I scrape off unruly ginger whiskers. They have grown up around the beard I keep on my chin. Though they warm my face, my cheeks are not used to them and itch constantly. I will be rid of them this morning.

I realize Brenna is not looking at the reflection.

"Do not stare at me."

"You should cut your hair," she says very softly. "Then Death will not recognize you. Mama would not cut her hair. So Death was able to find her."

Her face is set as if by a sculptor's hand. There is no girlish quiver of the lip or wetness in the eye. Her mother could have benefited from half her will.

The dagger feels suddenly light in my palm. I hand it to her.

"Here then. You do it for me."

I watch small handfuls of long matted hair fall onto the snow. She works quickly and surely. The air is cold on the back of my neck. I feel like a shorn sheep, the years of my neglected hair in clumps all around me. It looks as if a fox has been torn apart.

She gives me back the dagger, eyes still solemn. "It is a good disguise for you."

I put my hand to the back of my head and feel uneven stubble and wisps of longer hair that somehow escaped her notice. I do not look at my reflection in the metal disk. Some handiwork is best left unseen.

21

That day, we finish the food Brenna packed, as well as the lentils I brought with me from Ansberg. Brenna cooks them for breakfast in my little pot. I forgot to bring a spoon, so she stirs the brown mush with my knife. We wait for the porridge to cool, then eat it with our fingers.

Brenna finds no hares with her bow as we travel. When night comes we are hungry again, and cold. Dark purple clouds advance across the sky like a funeral procession, threatening snow.

The road is through open land, and it is hard to find a place sheltered from the night winds. I realize I am shivering a little as Brenna builds a campfire for the night.

I sit before it, cross-legged and in a poor mood from my empty stomach.

She is doing something with her father's traps. I could not say what, for I have no knowledge of the craft. But she kneels beside me, diligently working to untangle a jumble of ropes and toothy steel bits.

Then she stands and wanders off, farther from the road. I watch her, no more than a brown mouse to my eye, as she circles our camp from a long distance. Every several paces she stops, kneels in the snow, and sets a trap. I wonder what she thinks she will catch. I would not know.

She is a useful creature, though. At least now there is the hope of catching food, and the fire she has built burns strong despite the wind.

Before the plague came to Ansberg, I had only ever spent one night like this, out in the wild and far from the Scharfrichter's home and the assurance of a warm bowl of Tante's stew. Jorg and I had wandered too far in search of Schlusselblume, their pale yellow flowers rare for that time of year. The man who raised me—ah, our father—needed to replenish his store of the plant, to dry the petals and then grind them into fine powder to mix into the drink that I, as Loewe for him, would give to the condemned.

Jorg and I knew better than to return home without the flowers. We would be beaten if we came home too late, but the beating would be all the worse if we arrived empty-handed. So we wandered far up into the hills and meadows, so steep in places that even the nightsoil workers' bony goats stayed away.

At last we found the sun-colored blooms, and enough to make the Scharfrichter lenient, perhaps, when he punished us for dawdling. But the sun was already low, and we without lanterns. Navigating the steep scree-covered slopes and rocky meadows would be foolhardy in the dark.

I had not even a flint with me then, nor a cloak, for it was only late summer. The air turned cold enough when the sun set. Jorg broke his fits of shivering to lament our sure deaths by frostbite or starvation, if the wolves did not find us first.

His cries only increased when I tried to quiet him with the back of my hand. At last I used the rope that held up his trousers to hog-tie him, his shirt pulled up over his trembling mouth. Only then did I manage to sleep in reasonable peace.

I needed to rest that night, for we would have to be home soon after dawn. Were I not back by the time the Scharfrichter woke and roused himself with drink, he would beat me thrice as badly. Or, in my absence, he would raise his hand to the next best thing: Elise and her infant girl with hair the same shade as her father's.

Brenna is not much older than Jorg was when he and I made a poor camp in one of the high meadows that night. I am lucky it was she I found, capable as she is, and not another helpless simpleton.

She returns to the warmth of the fire. All at once she drops into my lap. I grunt in surprise. She rubs her head against my chest, snuggling into my cloak like the cat Elise kept as a pet, until my father decided he needed it in the Falterkammer.

I stare down at her. Even Sabine, spoiled by the women, whining, constantly underfoot, kept a little distance from me. Perhaps Brenna fears nothing. She pulls up the edges of my cloak around herself, intending, I think, to sleep on top of me.

"When Papa and I camped, he would tell me wonderful stories," she murmurs into my shirt. She looks up at me, waiting for something.

I yawn.

"Will you tell me a story?" she asks, a little impatient.

I am silent for a long time. "I do not know any stories."

"Really?" She is shocked. She sits up a little. "Shall I teach you some?"

"No. You should sleep." And be quiet so that I may do so, as well.

She frowns up at me, but falls silent. I do not know what to do with her, her weight all on my legs and me sitting up. I cannot sleep this way. I shift to one side, trying to get her off my lap so I can stretch out on the hard ground.

She is like a dead weight, clinging to me as I lean to one side and the next, trying to dislodge her.

Finally I pick her up and lay her beside me. She opens one eye.

"You would not be so restless if you knew stories to make you sleepy at night," she says in a chiding little voice.

I ignore her as I lean back onto my pack to ease my travel-sore muscles. The cold leather and wood give little comfort.

"Papa knew so many stories that he could tell them all night and into the next day—"

"Tell a damn story if you like, girl."

Brenna leans against me again, quiet. The tone of my voice must have discouraged her. Good. I am too tired to listen to a little girl's chatter.

I shut my eyes and try to focus on the warmth of our little fire, on the heat of the small, plump body pressing against my chest. Even with all the cloaks and bedding we brought from the trapper's home, the cold finds its way to my skin. It is going to be a long, bitter night.

"Papa said every star in the sky was the campfire of an angel—"

I open my eyes. Brenna is muttering, as much to herself as to me.

"Because when angels travel down from heaven, they get cold at night, too, just like us. But their fires are brighter, and warmer than ours, and the flames burn green and pink and silver—"

So, I am not spared her chatter after all. It is low enough not to bother me much. I let her ramble on.

The wind must be dying some, for I feel a little warmer.

The plaguewalker is sleeping. She is curled on the snow, cloak a swirl of red over her. Now I can catch her before she rises and starts ahead of me again. I grab the edge of her cloak.

It is nothing but the shorn fur of a fox. The wind snatches it from my fingers. Then I look up, and see her at the opposite edge of the field, her back to me. She is walking quickly, ever closer to where white snow meets gray sky.

"Damn!"

I sit up, startled.

Brenna is standing a few feet away. Her nose is bright red from the cold.

A tangled pile of traps lies in a heap at her feet. I see blood and a tear of red fur on one of the toothed metal pieces.

"We nearly had a damn fox," she says, indignant. She gives the trap a little kick.

I wipe my eyes and look around our camp. It snowed a little last night. But the air seems warmer than it has been for several days.

I stand, wobbling a little. The hunger is starting to eat at my head, making me dizzy.

"We walk."

Brenna scowls at me. I suspect she is no less hungry than I. But there is no point in standing here, pouting over her failed traps. We gather our things and set off along the road, following the path Sabine left in my dreams. But she is so far ahead of us.

Neither of us speaks all that day and into the next. I have nothing to say, and hunger has dulled Brenna's desire for chatter. She clings sullenly to my back. Were it not for her warmth against my shorn head, I would think I was carrying nothing but a pack.

The morning of that second full day without food, I think I am dreaming. Even with my eyes open, kneeling on the snow to roll up our blankets for travel, I think I am still asleep.

Or perhaps hunger has dulled my senses. I cannot believe that what I see is real.

I do not mention it to Brenna. I do not want her to think I have gone mad.

Ahead of us on the road, the clouds are thin and dark, shifting with the wind. But they are moving the wrong way, upward instead of across the sky.

Brenna sees I am looking at something. She follows my eyes.

"A town!" she shouts, and waves at the black snake clouds.

I blink. Of course, a town. And one with many chimneys.

The hunger has affected me. It takes several moments for me to understand. Morning hearths do not light themselves, nor can ghosts do the task. The town ahead of us is large, and alive, filled with bakers, butchers, vintners, brewers, cheesemakers...

"Hurry!" Brenna shouts at me over her shoulder. She is skipping along the road.

I see then that the road dips ahead, down into a valley. Across the valley floor, not an hour's walk, is the town. It rises on an easy slope, hidden to us until now. A reddish stone castle sprawls like a lazy guard on a ridge above the town.

I pause at the crest, Brenna slowing a few paces ahead. Six roads lead into the town, which has overflowed its walls and spills into the valley. I see wagons and carts laboring through the snow on five of the roads. Market day, then. Farmers and trappers haul their goods to sell from nearly every direction.

The sixth road, on which we stand, bears no wagon ruts in the snow. No one has traveled it for days.

Brenna runs down into the valley, her short legs clumsy through the snow. I am a little slower behind her. The hunger makes my footing unsteady. She waits for me where the roads merge into one approach to the town.

A farmer hunched over the reins of his scrawny team looks down at us from his wagon. He spits into the snow.

"Traveling on the Arbach road?" He narrows his eyes. "We'd heard the dying had been that way."

He is looking at me, waiting for a response.

"It is no more." Arbach is no more, I think to myself. And the dying is gone from there. There is nothing left to die.

We fall into step behind his cart, which I see now is mostly empty. A few sacks of something, apples perhaps, sit near the front of the cart. I glance at Brenna and see she is staring at the bags, licking her lips.

Behind us, three men on foot carry several deer skins over their shoulders. And on their heels is a man hauling a sled piled with raw wool. Soon we are but two in a long line of vendors and buyers filing into the town.

Guards stationed on either side of the Haupttor give me a second glance as I pass under its shadow. One gestures to me.

"You there, step aside. Over here." The guard motions.

I obey. He looks me up and down.

"We watched you and the boy come down from the Arbach road," he says slowly, frowning at me. "What's your business here?"

I am used to asking the questions, in the familiar shadows of my workroom. It takes me a while to realize through the haze of hunger that he is waiting for me to answer.

"We will buy food—"

"Have you money?" He looks over Brenna and me. I can imagine I look as road-weary and poor as she. "For thieves and pickpockets are not welcome here. Nor are bearers of the plague. Let's have a look at what you bring."

So that is it, then. I think of Jorg's stories of the other incarnation of the plaguewalker, not the maiden in her red cloak, but the tall man in black. No wonder they are so suspicious.

I have no money. I had not yet given thought to how Brenna and I would buy food. I set my pack down and lean over it, loosing the ties. Bright blue silk shines up at me from an open-mouthed sack.

"We will sell this," Brenna says suddenly. She stands at my side. I feel her hand on my arm.

"And where did you get that?"

I brush the shimmering fabric with my gloved hand, and think not of the desperate maid who brought it as payment to me, but of Sabine. "It was for my daughter."

Perhaps my voice was softer than I thought, but the guard leans forward as if to hear better. His brow furrows, but not in anger. It is pity.

"The dying came to Arbach, but we were not there," Brenna continues, distracting him with the brightness of her tone. "Papa and I are trappers."

The guard nods at her, glancing at me again. Trappers give little thought to their appearance. I see him working her words over in his head, deeming them acceptable. He waves us on and turns back to the line of people passing under the Haupttor.

I tie shut the flap of my pack again. Brenna is watching me closely with an expression much like that of the guard.

"You look very sad when you speak of Sabine," she says thoughtfully. "We must find her for you."

I shrug, uneasy at the earnest look on her face. The maid in my dreams is so small now, barely a red speck ahead of me on the road, like a single drop of blood.

I stand, and feel Brenna's chubby fingers slip into mine. I look down at her, surprised again. She has a strong little grasp.

Her eyes are already moving further along the crowded alley. She walks a little in front of me, almost pulling me along.

The crush of so many people is new and unwelcome to me. I am used to people avoiding me, pressing themselves against each other to leave a wide space wherever I walk. Here, people brush and bump against me. They look at me, too, eyes unafraid to meet mine.

Everyone is staring at me, I think. Suddenly I wish I had my mask again.

"You there! Move along!"

I look over my shoulder and see a man snapping the reins of his horses. The wagon behind him is piled with barrels.

"You, big man! Step aside and be quick about it!"

Brenna pulls me under the eaves of a shop. The merchant passes by, frowning at me.

"Have you never been to a town on market day?" she asks me, not chiding but with surprise. I glance down at her but say nothing. Tante did the buying for us, even before I was Scharfrichter. And as Loewe, my father's assistant, I kept to the alleys to which he was restricted. No one dared call out for us to move along.

"Ah, look!" Brenna tugs on my sleeve, looking into the open windows of the shop where we have paused.

It is a bakery. Someone unshuttered the glassless windows to let heat from its ovens steam out onto the street. Rows of fragrant breads and cookies line racks just out of our reach. Brenna licks her lips.

"Mandelbrot!" she whispers as if in prayer. "Oh, can we buy some? Please?"

I do not know what she is talking about. Tante never had coins to spare for sweets.

"Papa bought me some once, when he took me to market," she is gushing now, leaning against the windowsill. A fat woman inside looks up and frowns at her, waving her aside.

"Come, girl. First we must find ourselves money."

I pull her away from the shop windows like a dog from a bone. And then I realize I plan to sell the silk. I must, if we are to buy food. The silk I meant for Sabine.

Brenna follows on my heels. In the push and pull of the crowd, her fingers slip out of my hand.

I glance over my shoulder.

"I'm here!" she shouts, waving at me from behind a portly man.

I nod at her and move deeper into the crowd, toward the Marktplatz.

Everything here is noise and color. Stalls ring the square, and more snake up and down across its center. People are everywhere, their chatter making my head ache.

I smell meat, and feel my mouth turn moist and expectant. But first the silk. I see a row of merchants unloading mounds of fabrics onto tables, talking amongst themselves.

I take the silk out of my bag. It is a little rumpled from the travel, but lustrous still. They eye it curiously.

"How much?" I ask the nearest.

He glances at his neighbors. "Is this all you have? It is not much."

"Enough for a dress," I say, pushing it toward him.

"We have silk of our own, man, and more of it than that. See if a tailor will buy it."

They turn their backs. I roll the fabric back into my bag.

And only then do I realize Brenna is not at my side.

I turn around, eyes searching the crowd. She is nowhere to be seen.

22

"Girl! Where are you?!"

I call for her. Several heads turn to look at me, but none is hers. The whole crowd seems to shift like a sleeping dog disturbed by a flea.

I retrace my steps, shouting for her. People frown at the boom of my voice, the coarseness of my manner as I shove them aside. Where has the girl gone to?

One of the guards patrolling through the market approaches me. I see his bright red garrison tunic from one corner of my eye as I scan the crowd for Brenna.

"You there, move along. Stop shouting. Sell your wares or move on," he says in the tone of a man who hopes I will not listen. He wants an excuse to use his authority. He is a big man, not as tall as I, but broad enough and with a flattened fighter's nose. I glance at him and think of Gilg. This man has the same malevolent glint in his eyes. He moves closer.

"I am looking for a little girl, have you seen her? Short, with a shorn head like mine, dark eyes—"

"If you've lost your kin, that's your own problem." He is directly in front of me now, hands folded over his wide chest and eyes glowering. I know the expression. Gilg wore it when he was sober and looking to beat up prisoners. "Now move on, or I'll throw you to the Lockwirt for disturbing commerce."

To be thrown into one of the cells in the dank underbelly of the town's Rathaus is a small threat. It would be like going home.

But I am in no mood for a fight. Brenna must be found. I am tired of little girls running off on me.

I turn away from the man and continue my search.

"You, big man!"

What now? The tug on my sleeve is insistent, like Sabine's when she dared. I turn around and see a man wearing a velvet cap that is too small for his round head. He is like a poorly made wooden toy, parts all out of proportion to one another.

"The weavers say you're selling a bit of silk," he says anxiously. "How much?"

I show him the creased fabric and ask him to name a price. He taps his chin with one fat finger, thinking, then names a sum.

It is less than a thief's confession would fetch me in the Falterkammer. But I do not know fabric or its value. Nor am I skilled in bargaining. I never had need to learn.

I shake my head. My stomach rumbles at that moment, and loudly.

He raises his offer, but only a little. "You'll not find another buyer. There is plenty of silk to be had here, and none of it travel-worn."

I may not know much about silk, but I do know when a man is lying to me. I frown down at him. It was much easier to deal with people in the Falterkammer.

"Then why do you want to buy it, unless at a price fair only to you?"

He thought me a simple woodsman. His eyes run over me again, quickly. They linger for a moment on the pommel of my sword. He takes a step back. "Only out of pity did I make my offer. You'll not sell so ragged a cut of stolen cloth here!"

He backs off into the crowd, and I am alone again.

I am standing at the edge of the Marktplatz. The Rathaus looms before me, larger than the one I knew. Steps lead up from where I stand to an ornate grated door. A pair of red tunics stare down at me, unsmiling. I pull my cloak forward, to hide my sword, and hope I did so quick enough, before they started to wonder what a man like me was doing in the midst of their market.

The guards look elsewhere.

Low, slatted windows run along either side of the Rathaus facade, just above the foundations. No muffled cries or shrieks of pain issue forth from them. Perhaps the hearth in the Falterkammer is cold today.

Again I push through the crowd, silent now, but looking. I pass stalls of apples, onions, breads, and sweets that I have never tasted. I am not so aware of my hunger anymore, though it makes my head spin.

I do not see the people glancing at me as they push past, except to notice that none of them is Brenna.

"Over here! Here!"

How long she shouted before I heard her, I do not know. But I feel a sudden jolt of relief when I recognize the voice.

She waves to me from the end of a row of stalls. I fight against the flow of buyers and sellers to reach her.

Brenna's face is flushed, her eyes very bright. When I reach her, she jumps up and hugs me. I stagger back.

"Where were you, girl—"

"I found her, I found her!"

I set her down. "Found who?"

"When you looked so sad I knew I had to find her for you, so I went from stall to stall asking people and at first no one knew but then someone said yes, a girl like her had come to town before last market day—"

"Sabine?"

Brenna nods excitedly. "Come, come! The man selling wineskins says he saw her sweeping floors at an inn. It is close by, he told me where!"

She grabs my hand and pulls me with more strength than I expect. We turn off the Marktplatz and down a narrow alley. The buildings here are older, and some look near collapse.

The inn is located in a dirty courtyard, filled today with the carts of merchants who have traveled far enough for the market to sleep here before returning home. The red-painted door is half open. I smell stale ale and cabbage.

"Come on!" Brenna pulls me over the threshold quickly. I am too slow to react, and smack my head against the lintel.

Rubbing the pain from my forehead, I follow her into a dark space that is more a cave than a room. A fire burns low against the opposite wall. Tables, mostly empty now, and mismatched chairs are the only furniture. A few men sit slumped over tankards, though it is too early for much business.

A woman stirring a pot over the hearth turns at the sound of my head hitting the doorframe. She is the fattest woman I have ever seen, rolls of flesh piling one atop another. Her dress is too tight for her girth, and the broad expanse of her breasts threatens to rip open the fabric with every wheezed breath.

"No children here," she says, jabbing a thick finger at Brenna.

Suddenly Brenna is less eager. She steps behind me, taking in the drab room and its drunken customers.

I know what kind of place this is. There was an inn much like it in my town, where men could come for drink and other vices at any hour of the day. My father saw it closed, invoking the law that allowed for the Scharfrichter alone to offer whores. He hadn't liked the competition.

And now I dread finding Sabine here.

"I am looking for a girl of some thirteen years. Tall, with green eyes and bright red hair."

The woman draws closer. She squints at me. I do not think she sees more of me than a tall shadow in her doorway.

"You've very specific tastes. Pity. We had just such a girl to satisfy you, but she's run off."

"When? Where?"

She shrugs and spits onto the filthy floor. "No matter. I've plenty young ones, if that's what you want."

I hate her. I do not want a whore to lie with. I want my daughter.

Brenna shrieks when I grab the woman by the shoulders and shove her back onto one of the tables. One of the drunks nearby rouses himself to watch the show.

Now I am leaning over her, close enough that she must recognize the flat green-gray of my eyes. Sabine's eyes. The whoremonger's garlic breath is overpowering.

I do not show my rage, though it threatens to boil over. I am in my Falterkammer again, and I will find out the truth. My voice is calm, steady, but she hears the anger behind it.

"Tell me, hag, when she came, how she left. Tell me or I will feed you to the fire in pieces."

She is breathing hard, but does not struggle. Her eyes dart around the room. "I've done nothing against you, man, she came on her own, fleeing from a cruel Scharfrichter was all she said, hungry and road-weary—"

"What did you do with her?!" I slam her back onto the table when she tries briefly to stand. She hits her head against the hard wood and groans weakly.

"She offered to keep the place clean. I took her in, out of kindness I tell you. I've enough girls in my stable already, didn't need another, though she was fair enough to bring the men in—"

I shove her down again, harder this time. I can feel control of my temper cracking.

"She stayed but a few nights. I'd thought she'd not balk at the men, seeing as how she'd been in the service of a Scharfrichter already. But when a few went for her, she fought 'em. Bit. Clawed. Nearly took out the eye of one. Took three of them to hold her down. Not many are willing to pay for that—"

I cannot speak. Fury is choking me.

Behind me, Brenna starts to whimper.

"Where is she gone to?" My voice does not sound human. I want to take this monstrous woman and stuff her into the pot that hangs over her hearth, until her fat boils over and there is nothing left but bone.

"I tossed her out!" she shouts back. "She was of no use, wild like an animal as she was. You're the Scharfrichter, aren't you, come to look for her? Well, you can have her! She fled town is all I know—"

"Which road?"

"The Devil if I know!"

I stand. The dizziness sweeps over me. Sabine, Sabine. I cannot think coherently.

"Please, let us go!" It is Brenna. She tugs at my sleeve, tears spilling onto her reddened cheeks.

The woman rolls off the table and starts to run for a door beside the hearth.

"FRANS!" she bellows.

I do not want to meet Frans. I do not want to linger a moment longer in this pit. The close air turns my stomach.

Brenna half-drags me out into the courtyard. She is ashamed. It was she who brought me here, to the whoremonger. Better that we had stayed in the Marktplatz.

I hear a man's rough voice behind me. Then I am stumble-running behind Brenna, clumsy with the weight of my pack. I do not want to brawl. I don't know how. And though I carry a sword, I know how to use it for only one thing.

So we run. I follow her blindly, away from the Marktplatz, away from the inn, into a maze of nameless alleys and buildings shuttered against the cold.

At last hunger trips me. I tumble and come to a rest against a pile of refuse. My head hurts.

She falls to her knees beside me, still crying. "Oh, she was horrible! What a wretched woman! We will never find Sabine now!"

I let her crawl onto my lap and cry out all her tears. I am afraid to stand, afraid that my legs will not hold me. I lean back and stare up at the dark gate ahead of me.

It is the rear gate of the city. I see familiar symbols carved onto the stone overhang. Two ravens, flanking a skull. The Rabentor.

I cannot see past the shut gate, but imagine well enough that here too stands a Rabenstein, a gibbet, rows of unmarked graves. And I can guess that beyond it lies a narrow trail in the snow, used by only one man and his family.

I stand slowly, hesitantly, and turn my back on the gate. I do not want to see what lies past it.

"Where are we going?" Brenna asks, wiping the last tears from her ruddy face.

"We are leaving this place. I will buy some food, and then we will leave."

We find our way back to the Marktplatz. Now Brenna clings to me as if she expects wolves to rush out at us from all directions. I go like a beggar from stall to stall, offering the silk. A fair-haired woman selling turnips looks it over. Her daughter beside her, a year or two older than Sabine, touches the fabric in delight and awe, as if it were God.

"My girl weds in the spring," the mother says with pride. "This would be a dress far finer than we'd hoped for her."

She offers me but half the sum of the man with the small cap, some of the payment in turnips. I nod. I cannot bring myself to speak.

She takes the fabric, smiling. Her daughter's eyes shine. Then I think, it is good that the poor farmer's girl will have a fine dress. Someone should.

"Here." I give a coin to Brenna. "Go buy your sweets."

"Where are you going?" Her eyes are very wide.

"I will buy bread. And then I will ask the guards at each gate if they noticed Sabine as she left."

Brenna hands me back the coin. "I will come with you. I do not want the Mandelbrot anymore."

I nod. She is sick at heart too, I think, over a girl she has never met.

"Come then. We should be gone from here soon."

I spend some of the coins from the silk on a few loaves of bread, still steaming from the oven. Brenna tucks one loaf into her shirt to warm herself as we walk along the inner perimeter of the town's walls.

I keep my sword hidden to avoid questions. It is easy enough, for long though the blade is, it disappears into the folds of my heavy cloak. At each guard post I stop to ask for word of Sabine. None is to be had. The men shake their heads and then turn their backs to us, more interested in monitoring the steady flow of buyers and sellers than helping a haggard, beggar-dressed man and child.

I want to ask them how it is, if they keep such close watch over all who pass in and out of the town, that they might have missed so fair a young woman. But I say nothing, lest my words bring me more grief. I have enough at the moment.

"That's him, all right!"

I hear the gruff shout only a moment before someone grabs me from behind. Brenna shrieks. I throw off the first attacker only to feel my pack being wrested off my shoulders, my arms held by hands that seem to multiply even as I struggle to free myself.

A man swears loudly, and I hear the sharp slap of a leather gauntlet against flesh. Brenna screams again.

"Little bastard bit me!"

"Karl, help me with this one!"

I try to twist around and see what has happened. Everything around me is colored like blood, from the red tunics swarming all over me to the ruddy faces of the guards trying to pin me.

One of them bangs the flat of his sword hard behind my knees. I crumple to the ground. A boot at my shoulder pushes me down farther, and I taste muddy snow as my face slams into a street gutter.

"Get his sword, then tie 'em up!"

The boot pressing me into the gutter eases a little then. I am able to turn my head and see that they have stripped Brenna of her pack.

Her face is very pale, but for a red welt across her mouth where the guard's gauntlet found home.

"We have done nothing," I say as someone knots heavy rope too tight around my wrists.

"Disturbing commerce, assaulting a merchant—and a woman, at that!" My captor turns me over on my back with a well-placed kick. I look up into the face of the brutish guard who cautioned me as I shouted for Brenna in the Marktplatz.

"I am only looking for my daugh—"

He silences me with another kick. I taste blood and feel a sharp pain in my jaw.

"At least let the girl go. She has done noth—"

He kicks again, this time in my ribs. "Shut up, beggarman. Another word from you and I'll have you watch as I beat the little biting brat till it's dead."

They haul me up and jostle me forward, back into the town. Brenna is ahead of me, a guard on either side of her. Two more lead the procession, carrying our packs.

The crowd that has gathered mutters as we pass. I see a familiar face at the front of its shifting, mumbling mass. The fat whoremonger is grinning, satisfied like a cat that has happened upon a bird with a broken wing. She spits at me as we pass. Her rolls of flesh quiver with every belly laugh.

They lead us to the Rathaus, around to its rear entrance. The devil-eyed guard leaves my side for a moment to unlock a heavy grate that serves as a door to the prison.

I look at the guard now nearest me. He glances up.

"Please," I whisper. "Do not take the girl down there. It is no place for a child."

His light eyes run over Brenna for a moment, then turn cold. He turns partway from me and says nothing.

The grate swings open. Brenna takes a step back as its shadow darkens the snow at her feet. She twists around to look at me. I stare at my feet and do not watch as they half-drag her down the stairs. Then it is my turn.

As they push me over the threshold, my head and shoulders stooped, I smell it. The familiar stench of darkness and misery would seep into my clothes, my hair, even my skin when I spent long hours in my Falterkammer.

I know the dimly lit stairwell as if it were my own, the earth-hewn steps leading steeply down into a stone room fetid with old blood and shit.

Brenna whimpers then, and shrinks back from the stink of the prison. The guards shove her forward.

I had forgotten how putrid the stench could be. It turns my empty stomach.

So, I am home again. Or in hell. Perhaps both.

23

The jail is larger than the one where Gilg and I worked. The bottom landing of the stairs opens into a circular room, with several corridors branching off in all directions like spokes on a wheel. Along the wall, the builders fixed pairs of iron cuffs. A withered man is chained to a set off to my right. He is naked and covered with sores. I recognize them as scourge marks left untended and open to infection.

Then I realize he is dead. His eyes are open and unfixed.

"What's the old man doing here, still?" one of my captors asks the guard who met us at the bottom of the stairs.

"Family can't pay up for burial. Meister Lockwirt said to let the bastard rot here then." The guard grabs Brenna and starts to chain her to the pair of cuffs beside the dead man. "It's been two days already, and I'm ready to put a torch to him myself. The stink makes me puke."

Brenna is breathing like a wounded hare. Her eyes are fixed on the corpse, her jaw chatters. The guard does not notice.

"Please, don't cuff the child there, beside a—"

The pommel of a sword smacks against my head and knocks me to my knees. Everything is spinning. For a moment I feel as if I am upside down, my head submerged in a barrel of pitch. I fight off the daze.

"I told you, big man, to keep your mouth shut." The monster's ruddy face passes before me, leering. He is headed over to Brenna.

"What's this?" A new voice joins us. It belongs to a wide, short little man with lank brown hair. He comes out of the shadows of one of the corridors, wiping his mouth. I smell ale and onions on him.

The big guard tells him of our alleged transgressions. It is the Lockwirt, then. He nods and smacks his lips, routing idly through our packs. His eyes linger on my sword, leaning in its scabbard against the wall. His fat little fingers wrap around the grip. With a grunt he unsheathes the blade and hefts it up to eye level.

It is too heavy for him. After a brief inspection he lets it clatter to the floor. The shrill clang of metal on stone makes my broken head throb.

"How is it a beggar carries a Scharfrichter's sword? Shall we add thievery to your list of crimes?"

There is more curiosity than menace in his voice. He waves off the garrison guards as his own assistants move forward to flank me. I am still on my knees, weighed down with dizziness, the room around me trembling with every breath.

"It is my sword. I was Scharfrichter at Ansberg." The words taste acrid in my bloody mouth.

"You? Dressed in rags? Bare-faced and begging in our streets? A liar and a thief, then!" He laughs lightly, as if a wench had tickled his ear with some bawdy whispering.

The guards snicker, too. I glance up at Brenna. She is unaware of me or of the men's guffaws. She stares at the rotting man beside her.

"Could you not free the girl? She has done nothing—"

"A little pickpocket, probably," jeers the jailer. "Or perhaps she is your assistant, your Loewe?"

This sends the men into another fit of laughter.

"What is all the revelry then?" comes another voice, from farther down one of the corridors.

"Ah, Meister Scharfrichter!" shouts the Lockwirt. "Have you finished your meal? Come then, join us. We have someone for you to meet! A colleague!"

The guts of the guards on either side of me shake and wobble with cruel laughter. The motion deepens my nausea. My Falterkammer, even Gilg's dark lair, knew no such foolishness. The shadows beneath the Ansberg Rathaus were a place of punishment and confession, not merriment. For these men the jail is only a diversion, a way of passing the time before their nightly dice games and drinking.

I wonder then if these were the men who visited the fat woman's brothel, who brutalized my daughter. The rage is welling up in me. I cannot stop it. I will rip them all to pieces, with my own teeth if need be.

Brenna sniffles. I glance over and see she is looking at me. She chews her lip, eyes wide.

The wave of anger passes over me and fades. To attack now, injured and bound and not much of a brawler to begin with, would be stupid. Even if I could take all three men, the sound of a skirmish would alert other guards likely lurking elsewhere in the jail. They would be upon me in moments.

A fourth man joins us then. He is bare-chested, and so badly bow-legged that he does not walk so much as roll from side to side.

His mask of office is not as elaborate as was mine or my father's. It is fitted close to his head, made of studded black leather. The only embellishment is a pair of stiff bat ears standing up from the crown. His light eyes study me with sharp interest from the mask's eyeslits.

The mouth of the mask is cut wide, but over the opening is a latticework of wire, like a fine grate. It gives him a permanently startled expression.

Brenna gasps at the sight of the executioner.

The man ignores her. He cocks his head at me. As the Lockwirt recounts my crimes with an occasional chortle, the executioner circles me. He looks me over from all angles, eyes lingering on my face.

"Stand him up."

Two pairs of arms hoist me to my feet. The sudden motion makes everything spin again. I stagger and would fall if the guards did not hold me.

The Scharfrichter circles again, close enough that I can see the wrinkles around his eyes and a gray beard fringing the bottom of his mask.

He stands in front of me, hands on hips. He is tall for a man, but not as tall as I.

I meet his gaze evenly.

"Martin."

I blink. At first I think he is calling for one of the other men, but then I realize his eyes are fixed on me alone, as if expecting a reply.

"No? Matthias?"

My own mouth works for a moment, unsure if this is going to turn into some joke for the amusement of the others. "My name is Marcus."

"Ah, yes, Marcus! I knew it began with an 'M.'" He nods in satisfaction.

"You do not know me?" His tone is easy, as if we were old friends meeting by chance at the Marktplatz. "Ah, but you were young. No more than four or so when last I saw you."

He gestures to the guards, who are not laughing anymore. All of them, even the jailer, look uncertain. "Untie him, then. He is surely the son of the Ansberg Scharfrichter. With his mother's coloring, but his father's bulk and manner."

I feel the knots at my wrists loosening, and then the sting of air on my skin where the rope rubbed me raw. And for once I am glad to be a Scharfrichter and to be recognized as such.

"Will you not free the girl?"

The Scharfrichter looks from me to Brenna and back again. He gestures to the Lockwirt.

Brenna runs to me and hides her face in my cloak, trembling. I let her lean against me but say nothing. We are not free yet. I am certain of nothing, especially the casual manner of the man before me.

Their fun gone, the jailer and his men back away from us, into the shadows of one of the corridors.

"So, your father, is he still the bastard he has always been?"

The question does not surprise me so much as the light tone of his voice. I tell him of my father's end. He nods.

"Did he never mention I was his Loewe, before you were born? I worked for eight years under him, till I learned of an opening here. It's a bigger place, with better pay. We've three Loewes here, you know, and plenty of work for all of them. That's how I started out. The last Scharfrichter had no sons. When he died, the mask passed to me."

I say nothing. The man chatters like a woman. No wonder he did not get along with my father.

"And, your father's sister, Anna." He pauses then. The bantering note in his voice fades. "Did she ever marry?"

It takes a long moment for me to understand he must mean Tante. I never heard anyone call her anything but aunt. "No."

He nods to himself. "A fine woman. Well-built. And with all the goodness that her brother lacked."

Behind his words I hear something else. I never thought of Tante as anything but the woman who made my meals, kept the house in order, and cooed to her precious flowers in the garden. There is enough in the man's voice to tell me he knew her differently.

"Does she never mention me?" He asks this a little too quickly.

I should tell him she is dead. It is the truth. But I hold back. I shrug noncommittally.

"I courted her for years. She would've married me, but for your father. Said he needed her about to keep things tidy. Then, after your mother died, he needed her to take care of you. I gave up after a long while. But, you say she never married, eh?"

I see interest and perhaps a boyish hope bright in his eyes. Surely it would spoil his good mood to learn of her death. Ah, Tante, if you are somewhere where you can hear this, forgive me.

"No. She spoke of a man she loved, but never gave name to him. It must have been you."

Tante never spoke of anything other than how much flour she needed to buy at market, or whether rats had overrun the cellar again. If she gave thought to this man, she did not voice it.

His eyes shine, taking in the lie greedily. "Of course it was me. She has aged well?"

I nod.

This pleases him. "She always was a fine woman."

"I was on my way back to Ansberg," I say then. A lie started is easier to finish than to tear down and rebuild with truth. "When I got into this trouble. She will be nervous if I do not return."

The man nods sagely. "She always did dote on you. Even wanted to take you along, raise you as our own when we married. Your father spoiled that plan, of course."

I nod again.

"Well then, all this trouble is over you looking for your little girl? Is this not her?" He points at Brenna.

I shake my head, and tell him instead of Sabine and her brief but terrible stay at the fat whoremonger's inn.

He clucks his tongue. "Ah, my sister-in-law."

I bite back the rest of my bitter words toward the innkeeper.

"No matter," he says, laughing when he sees my sudden regret. "You can say no worse than the truth of her. She and my wife were daughters of the old Scharfrichter. I had no taste for the trade and let her take it over. I will have a talk with her. She is surely mistaken that you attacked her."

He stiffens suddenly, his whole body gone rigid with a new thought.

"My wife is dead. You must tell Anna that," he says in a rush. "It was a marriage just to please the Scharfrichter, and to secure my own future. She bore me a son, but neither lived beyond the birthing bed. I did not take another wife. Anna will understand."

I nod. And in my mind I begin to peel off the layers of years around Tante. She was still young when I was little. She had the same black hair as my father, and was tall and slender. She was indeed a fine woman, before the years of hard work wore her down.

"If I let you go on my word, and see you leave town at once, the Lockwirt will not be too upset," he continues. "And I will say nothing of a Scharfrichter walking our streets, through our Marktplatz, I hear, and bare-faced, too. I will consider that you are visiting Wuerzberg as a distraught father, and forget that you have broken more than one law."

Then I think he winks at me.

"Our cells are full at the moment, anyway, and as you might imagine we've no place to put the wretches already here, let alone new prisoners." As he speaks he gestures to the dead man chained beside us.

I glance down at Brenna, still burrowed into the folds of cloak, hugging my leg. She has not yet stirred.

"I will tell Tante—Anna—of your kindness, and give her your regards."

His smile is wide enough for me to see his yellowed teeth. "Good. Perhaps I will pay her a visit, after the winter."

I nod. "You would be welcome."

He does not need to know now, I decide. If he makes the trip after the thaw, he will find the grave behind our house and think that the plague struck after I returned, perhaps. Let him live a few more months before knowing the truth.

I want to ask then for some bread, for some bandages to bind the hot, aching places where the guards left their mark. But I do not find the words. I do not want to linger a moment longer in this place, to accept the generosity of this man who sees fit to reminisce of lost love while the stench of death reeks all around us. I want to leave at once, before the smell cloys its way again into my clothes.

He lets us retrieve our packs and my sword, then calls the Lockwirt's men to escort us to the town gates. He walks with us as far as the top landing of the prison stairs.

Outside the prison, I welcome the thin winter air as it needles into my clothes to find my sweat-soaked skin. Brenna, who has been silent this whole time, sucks in the cold air like a man nearly drowned. Her tears begin again, but out of relief now. Her little fingers are trembling and damp with sweat as they slip into mine.

"Safe journey, then!" says the Scharfrichter to our backs.

I glance over my shoulder, but cannot bring myself to wave back. Instead I nod, and hope he does not see I am ashamed to have misused Tante's memory.

He laughs at me.

"Your father's son to the last, Marcus! Silent as the grave!"

24

The way out of town and down into the valley stretches before us. I stare at the roads that intersect with it a little ways ahead, each leading in a different direction.

The stink of the prison is fading, and with it my thoughts about my aunt's old love. Likely I owe my life to him and a lie. But now I can think only of what brought me so far from Ansberg. Ah, Sabine.

It is futile. I was a stupid man to think I could find her, when even in my dreams she travels each day farther ahead of me. And now she may be in any of a half dozen directions.

Better I had not looked for her. Better I had stayed in my own Falterkammer, rotting in the darkness.

"Which road will we take?" Brenna asks very softly. She nudges me when I do not answer.

"It does not matter," I say at last. My sigh huffs out in a cold, white cloud.

"But it does! We must try to find her!" She is tugging on my sleeve now like a monk on a bell rope. She is on the verge of tears again, her strong will worn down from the day's events.

I stand on the side of the road, staring at the gray horizon ahead of me.

"We will go this way," Brenna announces. She is pointing at the road that runs straight down the middle of the valley.

I shrug. It makes no difference. I will walk on the road as long as I can because I have nothing to draw me back to the place where I was born, nor anything to make me choose a better direction. Let the girl have her way.

I follow her to where the road she has chosen branches off from the others. If nothing else, it is easy walking. The snow here has been trampled flat, and even the little girl has no trouble tromping through it. We are well away from the town by the time darkness arrives.

Brenna is silent as we travel, walking close at my side. I glance down at her and see the fierceness of her expression. She watches the road ahead like a sentry warned of impending attack.

Feeling my eyes on her, she glances up. "I have seen dead bodies before."

I raise an eyebrow at the pronouncement.

"That man in that cellar...he was very ugly, that is why I stared." She frowns at me, trying to look as fearless as she pretends to be.

I nod back.

"I cried only because I saw them hurt you. I thought you were afraid." As she speaks, I see she is already reworking the day's events to let her remember them as less brutal than they were.

"I was afraid."

She looks interested at this, and a little relieved. I say nothing more to her of our time in the jail. Let her remember such things as she wishes. I suspect it is how she has survived the past few weeks.

We stop then for the night, in a little knoll to one side of the road.

Brenna builds our campfire and sets out one of the loaves of dark bread that I bought with the silk money. I watch her slice the bread but make no move when she offers me a piece. I have lost my appetite. Perhaps it gave up on me ever feeding it again, and wandered off in the snow.

She nibbles on a small piece, holding it close to her face like a squirrel with a nut. I do not like her staring at me as she eats. Sabine used to do that.

I turn away.

Then I am angry. The anger rises within me like floodwaters after a sudden thaw. I never raised my hand to Sabine. I kept her warm and well-fed. I was trying to find her a husband, perhaps not the finest man to be had, but the best she might hope for.

Now she has nothing, traveling the road by herself, vulnerable to even worse than that pig of an innkeeper. I think of the brutish men who would visit my father for drink and whoring when I was a boy, of the cruel slashes on Elise's and Claudia's backs after the Brethren had their entertainment. I think of the thieves who stole everything from

Brenna's home. Only because the girl was quick enough to hide herself and her mother were they spared, I am sure.

I sit there and think of all the ugliness in the world that Sabine rushed toward that midnight when she fled my home. And I who had never caused her grief.

"Please, do not look so sad," Brenna says suddenly.

I glance up at her, crouched in front of me. She moved around me when I turned so that she could stare at me still.

I turn away again and busy myself with the sack of herbs I have brought with me. Now that we are well away from the town, I have time to mix a paste of Salbei to soothe the bloody place in my mouth.

Brenna moves around me again to sit at my side. She watches me work for a little while and then thrusts both hands into the sack of medicines.

"What are you doing, girl?" I ask sharply.

She holds up one of the clay vials that I took from my cupboard. There is no fear in her face. "What's this?"

"Leave it alone. Get out of my things."

"Can I sprinkle it on the turnips and cook them in your little pot? Will they taste better?"

"I said leave it be, girl. Sniff enough of that and you'll sleep forever. It's only to be used in a poultice, over a stinking wound that has filled with pus."

She looks at the stoppered vial with new interest. Then she sets it aside and takes out another.

"And this?"

I shift so I am facing her. Had I the energy, I would reach over and grab the vial of dried Hopfen from her greedy little hands. "That's for pain."

"Do you eat it then?"

I shake my head. "Sprinkle a bit in some drink. It takes a very little to dull the pain."

She holds up a small vial marked with the word Blutwurz. "What does this do?"

"Calms an upset stomach. Stops the runs, if enough is taken."

She smiles at me suddenly. "You do know stories! You told me you did not, but each one of these is a story!"

I blink at her.

Now she is girlish and excited again, rummaging through my bag and asking me, always asking. What is this for? And this? How much of this? She begins to open the vials, carefully, and sniffs each one.

Then she finds the dark metal flask. She holds it up before her, cocking her head to listen as the spirit inside swirls and splashes when she shakes the flask. Her eyes turn thoughtful.

"Be careful with that. It is very strong, and so near the flames it can explode. It is a spirit, good in small doses for fever and chills. But too much will make a man stupid."

Her eyes turn on me, brow creasing over them. Her voice is suddenly without delight. "You told us this was holy water, to consecrate the ground for Hans' and Papa's graves."

Ah, yes. I had forgotten. She frowns at me, accusation on her rounded child's features more obvious than if she had shouted it.

I look away, at the fire. I have nothing to say in my defense.

She puts the spirit back into my bag, then carefully gathers all the others and packages them again as neatly as I had done. She says nothing, but I sense her disappointment.

So maybe now she will leave me too, running off in the night, preferring the cruelty of strangers to my company.

Her weight in my lap is sudden.

"Papa is in heaven anyway. God would not deny so good a man," she says, wrapping her cloak around her, and then pulling the edges of mine up over us both. "And we will find Sabine for you."

I am ashamed then. The girl has will enough not only for herself and her mother, but for me as well.

My appetite is with me after all. It makes a mewling noise then, muffled by her weight on my belly. I lean forward, careful not to disturb her, and reach for the bread she has left out for me. I will need my strength, I think, to keep up with her.

That night as I sleep, Brenna's breath warm against my neck, I do not dream of the plaguewalker.

I dream instead of a snow-covered field, stretching in all directions, unbroken but for a single set of footprints. They are big feet for a girl.

In my dream I do not follow them, but stand in the cold, staring at the horizon where the figure that made the prints has long since vanished.

25

We walk. We follow the road doggedly, into low hills, across flat fields that remind me of the endless empty stretch of land in my dreams, through forests where the animals are asleep for winter and do not make themselves available to Brenna's bow.

The bread I bought at market has hardened and is dry in the mouth. And there is little of it left. The handful of turnips given as part payment for the silk found their way into our bellies long ago. I still have most of the coin that the farmer's wife gave me to afford her daughter a fine wedding dress, but it is not much. It will buy food only for a few days more, and then only if we find another town.

My sword is the last thing of value that I have, and its value is questionable. No one would want to buy the sword of an executioner.

Brenna does not complain, but sometimes I think I see the worry on her face, same as mine. But she does not protest each morning when I shoulder my pack, and set out on the empty road, chasing ghosts.

Perhaps I am as mad as was her mother.

If we find Sabine, or if we do not find her, it no longer matters to me. I walk because I can think of nothing else to do. It seems I will spend the rest of my days wandering the roads, lacking occupation, begging for food. I know no skills, none of value outside the Falterkammer, anyway. And even if I should find employ in the next town, or the one after it, the first we find that has need of a Scharfrichter, I am not so eager to wear the mask again.

I am tired of it, of everything. I think it would be good if snows piled on top of us both in the night, leaving us to sleep forever.

The sound of laughter rouses me from my private Falterkammer. I glance up and see Brenna running alongside the road, kicking up sprays of snow. The drifts are few here, and she chose this morning to walk beside me rather than ride high on top of my pack.

She glances over her shoulder, grinning at something. I do not know what.

"Don't you feel it? It's nearly warm as spring!" She skips forward a little way and then spins around on her heel. Her short-limbed motions are jerky under the burden of her pack. Her laughter squeaks in the air.

It is warmer. I notice it only then. The sun has come out as we walked. The sky is clear for the first time in days. On either side of the road, melting icicles glitter as they thin into nothing from the branches of trees.

Brenna has pulled off her capuchon and twirls bareheaded on the road in front of me.

I wonder how she is so merry, how the deaths of her parents and brother, and the long days of cold and hungry travel, have not poisoned her. Perhaps it is because she is but a child and does not understand that nothing but the same lies ahead for us.

I frown at her then. There is nothing I can do for her. She is a wily, bright young thing, and I can offer her nothing, except perhaps the same fate that found Sabine.

"Why is it you never smile?" she asks, glancing back at me again.

"I have no cause to do so," I grumble back at her. And I wonder if it is better to face the world bright and expectant as she does, only to be disappointed, or if one should expect the worst from the first moment.

She raises her eyebrows. "Never?"

I shake my head.

"When we find Sabine, will you not smile even then?"

I sigh. I want to take her by the shoulders and tell her Sabine is far away by now, and if by the smallest chance we do find her, she will be but another mouth to feed, and I have no means of giving either of them shelter. Or anything else.

"Well, I will smile," Brenna says reprovingly. She warms to the idea. "I will smile and take her hand and we will live like sisters in a cabin in the woods, and I will hunt and trap and she will dry cherries like Mama used to, and you will take us to town on market day."

Then I see. The girl does not understand the word Scharfrichter. She does not know what I am.

I do not answer her. She continues to skip and dance along the road, her way easier now that the snow is melting. I watch her and feel an emptiness in my gut that has nothing to do with hunger.

The afternoon shadows are lengthening as we crest a hill, and see a walled complex lying ahead on the next rise of road. It is not a town, for it is too small. Nor is it a nobleman's manor. The wall is high and white, and over it I can see the tops of several white buildings, one of them with a bell tower. The whole compound caps the top of the terraced hill like a crown.

As we near I see a large cross on top of the tower. A monastery, then.

"What sort of place is that?" Brenna asks. "It looks like one of the castles in Papa's stories!"

The compound lies a little way off the road. She does not ask when I turn aside from our route and begin climbing a short trail up to its gate.

The iron gate towers over even me. It is locked. I peer past the bars and see a wide courtyard, overlooked by a two-story dormitory with arched windows shuttered for winter. Steady puffs of smoke rise from the chimney of an outbuilding beside the gate, and I think I can smell baking bread.

The place looks prosperous enough. Surely the monks will have food to spare for a man and girl traveling in the snow.

No one comes to greet us. No faces appear at the windows.

I lean forward to see the church entry. Its doors are closed. Nothing stirs.

"Hallo!" I shout.

A snowball whizzes past me and toward one of the windows. It makes a loud bumping noise off one of the shutters and then crumbles to the ground below.

Brenna throws another.

"Stop," I warn her.

But either my shout or her sure arm roused someone from within. A door at the bottom of the dormitory opens.

It is a woman coming toward us, clutching a grayish cloak closed against a light wind. Beneath it I glimpse white robes. Her hair is hidden under a white wimple and veil.

She is a little older than I, with pale eyes. Her cheeks are red from the cold, or perhaps discomfort. She stops a short way from the gate and looks us over.

She does not like the look of me, a giant man haggard from travel and hanging on to the bars of the gate like a child on its mother's skirts. But her eyes soften when she sees Brenna. Whatever I am, few brigands travel the roads encumbered with children.

"Peace of Christ be with you," she says slowly, as if her mouth has started to freeze. I can see she wants to ask what we are doing loitering outside the convent gate but cannot think of a polite way of doing so.

"And you," I say, hoping it is the proper address. With nuns I have had no dealings, but I assume they are as intolerant of Scharfrichters as are priests. "The girl and I are traveling, and would ask if you might spare some food. We have not much money."

She glances over us both again. "I will speak with the Mother. I am sure we can give you something."

"Can we enter, to sit in the kitchens, perhaps, just to warm ourselves?"

She frowns. "Men are not allowed on the cloister grounds, unless they are priests here to give the Sacraments, or are badly infirm."

I should have guessed as much. "Just the girl then? She has been walking a long way, and a rest would do her good."

Brenna pokes me in the side. "I'm not tired."

The nun looks between us. I can see her mind working over the sight of us, and wondering who we might be. For a moment her face pinches at me, as if trying to see details better. I realize that my cloak is caught on the pommel of my sword, and that she can see the skull engraved on the steel. I pull my cloak forward.

"I thought her a little boy at first," she says then, eyes turning back on Brenna. "She may rest inside, if she wishes."

The nun steps forward to unlock the gate. She is near enough now that I see the healthy shine in her full cheeks. She looks well-rested, content. I glance down at Brenna and see dark shadows under her eyes. Travel and hunger have lent a pallor to her face.

The thought comes to me all at once, like a punch in my empty belly.

"Might she stay here, to live? She is orphaned. Could you take her in?"

The woman looks between us again. "She is not your daughter?"

"No. I found her as I traveled. The way is hard for so young a child, and I have nothing to offer her—"

"NO!" Brenna shouts at us both, taking a step back in the snow. Her face burns red with sudden indignation.

I ignore her. It is right to do this. She would be assured of food and shelter here, and of protection from the wolves out in the world.

"She is a hard worker, and bright," I say quickly, over Brenna's wailing.

"I will have to talk with our Mother, but given the circumstances, I think—"

"NO! NO!" I feel her meaty little fists smacking into me. "I'm not leaving you!"

The nun frowns at her show of temper.

I grab her hands and twist her back and around, as I used to do with prisoners who considered resisting. Pinned with her back against my thigh, she kicks futilely, like a dog straining at the end of its tether.

"She has had a difficult time since her parents died, and is still upset over their loss," I explain quickly, lest the tantrum ruin her chance of acceptance. "She will calm soon enough given the proper attention."

Now the nun is frowning at me. For the way I grabbed the child, I can guess. She steps back, leaving the gate locked.

"I will ask our Mother, when I inquire what food might be on hand for you." She backs away from us as fast as her clumsy long robes will allow.

Brenna is bawling as I have not heard her since she fell behind me on the road the day after her mother's suicide.

I kneel in the snow so that I am at her level and turn her around to face me.

"No, I do not want to stay here, with strangers! I want to come with you to find Sabine, to live in our cabin in the woods!"

"Brenna, there is no cabin! And we are not going to find Sabine! She is lost to me, and I have nothing more! No food! No home!

Nothing!" I am louder than I intend, and regret my angry shout in her face.

Her features shudder with shock as if she heard a sudden noise. I know it is the sound of her child's dream collapsing.

She is hysterical now, wailing, quaking, throwing herself against me. I catch her, lest she tumble to the snow when her knees buckle.

"If I l-leave you," she stutters, sucking in too big gulps of air. "Then y-you will have no one to hunt for you. And you will starve."

"It is better for you here, Brenna." I manage to say this better, softer. "I will be all right."

She shakes her head at me. "No. You cannot even build a fire. I have seen you try. You do not know how."

I say nothing. It is true enough.

Her fingers wrap around my neck. "You need me to take care of you."

"The road is hard, and nothing but the same or worse lies ahead. It is not a place for a little girl."

She has stopped crying. Her eyes narrow for a moment.

"If you abandon me here," she says lowly, "I will run off like Sabine did, in the middle of the night, and you will never find me, but you will know that I did this because you left me."

I frown at her. I had forgotten what a wily thing she is. I do not doubt that she could find a way out of the cloister compound, or that she would try.

"You would be a foolish little girl if you did," I say, though I know my words carry little weight at the moment. She will have her way or else, consequences be damned. Ah, devious little girls.

The nun is crossing the courtyard toward us, a basket under her arm. Her eyes dart from one face to the next, taking it all in and guessing what has happened.

"Our Mother is willing to take the girl in. We have room. The dying reached us early in the fall, and we lost half our numbers. We are welcoming young girls willing to give themselves to Christ."

"I am not willing," Brenna says sharply, folding her hands over her chest.

I clear my throat. "Hush, Brenna. We thank you, but...I have decided she should stay with me."

The nun frowns at me again. I see an evil thought glimmer in her eye as she wonders about the big, rough-looking man traveling with a little girl not of his blood.

"She has become...like a daughter to me." With all the grief that comes with it, I add in my head.

The woman considers this. She nods. She lifts a cloth draped over the basket and holds it close to the iron gate so that I may take what is inside. She does not want to unlock the gate for me.

Brenna leans against me, looking into the basket and wondering why I make no move.

Eggs. There is bread as well, but all around the loaf are those detestable eggs.

"They are hard-cooked already, and will travel well."

I sigh. "You are too generous. Thank you."

Brenna reaches through between the bars and begins to pile the eggs into a sack. She is smiling, content to have her way.

I take the bread and hand it to her. The nun looks at us both for a moment, staring at me longer than I would think proper for a woman of the veil. There is a hint of recognition in her face. She must have guessed what I am, as readily as Brenna's mother had. She turns back to the convent.

"We will pray for you both."

26

We cannot travel much farther that night, for as we make our way from the convent back down to the road, the sun is setting. At least its warmth lingers, and it is not so cold.

We find a good place to camp at the bottom of a hill, between forest and a wide field. Brenna builds the fire.

The eggs fascinate her. She has never seen one.

"Won't my teeth break?"

"You must peel it first."

"Show me!" she demands, pushing two into my hands. I tap one and start to work off the brittle shell. Her jaw hangs slack in fascination.

I hand one to her, watching as she sniffs it and turns it around slowly, like a dog that has just found a new and curious scrap. Her eyes widen when she bites into it.

"Ooh, it is like cream, with butter in the middle!"

She devours it and takes the second out of my hand to try her skill at peeling it.

I smile down at her, the eager little egg-eater.

I have stopped dreaming of the plaguewalker, of her cold eyes and cloak the color of freshly spilled blood. I do not even dream of the empty field where her footsteps track toward the horizon.

Instead I think while I sleep, my mind so given to wandering now racing around itself to think of what I will do now, miles from the dead place where I was born, with Brenna to provide for.

I should find a town in need of a Scharfrichter, I know. That is the most logical choice. But I do not want to wear the hot mask, to walk where the town decides I may. I do not want to work each day with the likes of men like Gilg or my father, or even the laughing Scharfrichter of Wuerzburg. Nor do I want to want to force the misery of a Scharfrichter's daughter upon Brenna.

She stirs then, and I open my eyes. She is curled in front of me, both of us on our sides with the bedding from her home piled all around us. We need it. It has turned cold again in the night, and a little snow has fallen as we slept.

Perhaps we should go back, to the hovel where she lived with her parents and little brother. It is not so solidly built a place, but once there I will not have to worry about us freezing to death each night. And I will have time enough on my hands to see that the chinks in its rock walls are filled and its roof thatched anew. The winter will be lean, but perhaps I can learn to hunt and trap. She will teach me.

I consider this, knowing that to return to Brenna's home means abandoning my search for Sabine. I cannot do both. It is hard to admit failure, I who am her father.

Brenna is awake, eyes looking over the snowy field before us. It was dark when we came here last night, and neither of us appreciated the sight.

I sit up beside her and dust a fine new powder of snow off us both. She does not stir. I wonder what she sees.

Forest rings the flat field on all sides. Pines taller than any I have seen since leaving my home rise up in rows like soldiers at attention. And the new snow has softened everything. Even the pink light of morning has a weak, gauzy quality to it.

"Look, near that tree!" she whispers, pointing. There are a dozen trees in that direction. I squint but see nothing.

She stands up and unties her bow from the pack I have been leaning against.

I look again and see something moving around the base of a tree not fifty paces from us, along the edge of the field.

She creeps like a stalking cat, low to the ground and slow, one of her father's arrows already on the string.

She shoots, and I see the scrawny hare jump into the air. The arrow juts at a sharp angle from its back leg.

The wounded animal turns in a frantic circle, as if to dislodge the arrow. Then it bolts, dragging the dying leg.

"Damn hare!" Brenna shouts. She drops her bow and takes after the terrified animal as it skitters across the field, leaving a trail of blood.

I smile and shake my head at her determination. I should tell her to mind her tongue, for such language is not fit for little girls.

She runs surely for a girl, and one with short legs at that. I watch her pursue her quarry, growing small until she is not much bigger than the hare.

They are in the center of the field now. The wounded animal is slowing, weakening. Perhaps we will have meat for breakfast after all. Brenna catches up with it easily.

Then she slips. She slides several feet, snow spraying in all directions and revealing the ice below her.

My smile fades. The field is too flat, too smooth beneath the snow. My eyes trace its outline, obscured at first glance by the snow.

It is not a field, but a large pond.

Brenna stands, uncertain. The hare has stopped a few feet away and twitches on its side, its will exhausted. She starts toward it.

"Brenna!" My voice rumbles across the thin winter air to her. "Come back!"

We can live without the hare. I do not like her so far out on the ice.

She waves me off over her shoulder.

I hear what sounds like a man being dropped from the ceiling of the Falterkammer. The ice at the center of the lake is thin. The sound of it cracking is like bones breaking.

Then she is falling. The ice collapses under her and she disappears into a dark hole gaping in the snow like a new grave.

I shout for her, with no purpose. What good can it do?

"Help!" Her head bobs up from the black water for an instant. "I can't swim!"

Nor can I. I throw off my cloak and sword.

I run out onto the ice. It is thick enough, here near the shore, but slippery under the snow.

She screams again, arms flailing just above the surface.

I slide on the ice, then fall.

"NO!" She is fighting the water as ferociously as she once hurled snowballs at Death. I am near enough now, crawling on my hands and knees, to see anger and terror in her face.

The ice splinters below me.

I hit the water all at once. It is cold, so cold it feels like oil, coating me, weighing me down. My feet do not touch the bottom.

I suck in air when my head breaks the surface. All is spinning. I have forgotten where I am, how I got to be in the black water.

Her screams rouse me. She is still a way off. The splash of her arms sounds weaker.

I grab handfuls of water, trying to pull myself to her as if along a rope. My legs kick awkwardly, wanting to touch something solid but finding nothing. Slowly, I draw nearer.

My head goes under again. The water floods my eyes, my mouth, my nose. It roars in my ears.

It is I roaring. My hand grabs something wet and soft. Her cloak.

I have her now, whether by arm or leg I do not know. She is screaming still, but stops fighting. I feel cold little fingers clawing for a hold on my shirt.

"Please, please," she cries.

The weight of her on me sends us both under again. She kicks me in the gut by accident, and I draw in too much water all at once.

Now she is panicked. We both are.

When our heads break the surface we are both screaming. It sounds like rabid wolves howling.

I turn toward what I hope is the nearest shore, pressing her against me. It is hard to keep both our heads above the water.

I can feel nothing. I know I still have her only because her muffled sobs are at my shoulder.

I slam into a hard edge of ice. The edge of the hole then. I try to push her onto it. It crumbles before us.

I kick and flounder again to the edge of the broken ice. Again it breaks when I drag her onto it. She falls into the water once more, and slips from my grasp.

I am weakening. My lungs feel as if they will burst. I cannot see anything, though I know my eyes are open. The water is pulling me under again.

My vision is restored for but a moment. I see the shoreline, so distant, so white with the dark pines rising above it.

And I see the plaguewalker, in her red cloak, standing there. Her eyes are cold and dead. She is waiting.

Then I slip under the water again and all is black. I feel something moving against me.

Brenna.

Our faces break the surface in unison. She has stopped crying. Now she gulps in air like a newborn filling its lungs for the first time.

"Please." It is all she says.

Something is pulling me under. My legs are so heavy. I feel as if I am being dropped from the ceiling of my Falterkammer, weights dragging me down all the faster.

I grab hold of her again. And I kick four times, as hard as I can. I pop up above the black waters for an instant.

And I bellow like a mad bull with the effort, throwing her ahead of me. She screams, flying through the air and landing on hard ice, sliding nearer to shore. But I hear no splash. The ice holds her.

The effort is too much. I slip under the water again, deeper now. It is a long time before I rise to the surface again.

There is no surface. My head bumps up against ice. Have I been down here so long that the lake froze over again? I am confused, understanding nothing. My hands claw at the underside of the ice.

The water fills my mouth, my blinded eyes. I am not cold anymore. I stop fighting and begin to breathe the dark water.

Strange that I would think of the Jew in the Falterkammer, as he sat broken in will and body, acquiescing to confession. God does not want me, he had said, and the Devil is afraid I will overthrow him.

We shall see.

From somewhere far away I hear a high, keening wail. It is the plaguewalker, calling for me.

No. It is Brenna. Then I realize she is not sobbing in terror. Her cry is one of loss and grief over me. Over me.

And then I do not want to find out if Heaven or Hell or nothing awaits me. Not yet.

I punch the ice once, twice, hard as I can. Then my fist hits nothing but air. My head rises with it, and the water sprays out of my mouth.

I find the jagged edge of ice and kick myself onto it. It holds, though my legs dangle in the black water behind me.

I swing one leg up onto the ice as if I were mounting a horse. Then I roll, free of the water, onto the thick ice near shore. I am lying on my back, staring up at nothing.

The air is so cold. I was warmer in the water.

She crawls to me from where I threw her, shivering. I feel her hands on my shoulders, trying to pull me toward shore. She fails, and sits there with my head in her lap, weeping.

I shut my eyes and know nothing more.

27

It is black, and hot. Hell, then. I hold my breath, waiting to see what demon will accost me first. I feel as if I am inside a furnace. Something is suffocating me. Am I wearing the Scharfrichter's mask again? It would be appropriate, here in Hell.

I cannot stop quivering. But it is not from fear. Rather it is as though I am sitting in an old cart drawn by too-fast horses, the road rough below us.

I breathe, and the air smells of an herb I should know by name. I cannot remember anything.

Someone is tying my hands. I feel them being crossed before me, and then rough fibers of rope scratching my wrists. I am being led to my own Rabenstein, then.

And suddenly I am curious to know if I will be beheaded or hanged. Women and nobles are beheaded. The lowliest of criminals are hanged.

I fall through nothingness. Hanged it is.

No. I hit ground, hard and cold. There is no noose around my neck. Something is poking at me from all sides, like animals snuffling over a carcass, looking for meat.

I am on my feet again, I think. I am sure of nothing.

For a moment the black turns to white. I look down at my hands, and see the rope. I am being led like an animal to slaughter.

The blackness returns.

I fall again, and again the wild animals prod at me until I am standing. All around me is black and spinning.

I want to pull off my mask. I am too hot. I reach for it and feel my own face. Has the mask been melted onto my flesh? I try to pull it off.

"Stop it!" my invisible demon escort chides me. It sounds like a very small demon, with a voice that squeaks a bit. I imagine a small brown mouse with horns and a forked tail.

I laugh like a madman.

"Stop it!" squeaks the mouse again.

I laugh harder. Then I stop, because it only makes me hotter.

I stumble again and hit my head on something hard. Harder than ground. I feel forward in the darkness and touch something cold, like a tombstone.

The mouse is chattering beside me, but I do not understand. It is too much effort to hear its words and figure their meaning.

Another voice joins it, then another. Women's voices. It is Tante, I think, and Gerta. I hear Elise above them all.

Now I understand. Hell for me will be the women's relentless chatter. I laugh again.

"It is the fever," Tante says. I feel something cold as death on my forehead. Skeleton fingers. "Can he stand?"

Several of the demon mice surround me, pushing, prodding, pulling me. I fall forward onto cold iron grating.

"By his cloak."

The mice roll me this way and that. Then as one they grab the bottom edge of my cloak and pull me feet-first along the ground. My head bumps up and down over every small dip and rise. My arms drag uselessly.

"Here. It will do."

The darkness clears again. I am in a small room, staring at a beam that runs across the ceiling directly above me. They brought me to the Falterkammer.

Someone is lighting a fire. Ah, no, please. I am hot enough.

Tante leans over me, her wizened features stern. I see the white funeral shroud in her hands. She draws it up over my face.

It is very cold, and for that I am glad.

How much time has passed, I do not know. It is very still. I hear only an occasional crackle from a fire, but I am no longer burning.

Something cool brushes against my forehead. I open my eyes.

She stares down at me, her fair features but inches from my face. I can feel her breath stir my whiskers.

The plaguewalker smiles, her mother's full lips curving more lovely than ever I have seen. And I notice that she has traded her blood-red plague cloak for one of white.

Perhaps I am in Heaven after all. What happened before must have been Purgatory. I wonder if they know I have not been baptized. I do not think I will mention it.

"Father?" she says very softly. "Do you know me?"

I try to nod, but my whole body has stiffened with death. I hope it is enough that I blink at her.

She turns slightly. I watch her dip a cloth in a bowl of water and wipe my forehead.

"Are you hungry?"

I wrinkle my nose, the most movement I can manage. I thought no one in Heaven was ever hungry.

I hear a noise on the other side of the room. It takes a moment for my eyes to focus on the open doorway and the woman standing within it.

It is not Tante after all, but a woman her age, with thin wisps of silver hair visible from under her veil.

"How is your patient, then?"

"Better," the plaguewalker says beside me. I hear an anxious note in her voice, as if she is eager for this woman's approval. "His fever is nearly gone."

The woman stands over me now. She is very tall, I think. Then I realize I am lying on the floor, thin bedding piled all around me.

"God be praised," she says. "I have never known someone to recover from so terrible a chill."

I stare up at her, and try to focus on her words. They make me dizzy. "I am not dead then?"

She shakes her head at my rasping voice.

I look over at Sabine. "And you are not a dream?"

"No, Father," she whispers, touching my forehead again to see if the fever is returning. "Though you were very nearly dead when the little girl led you here. She said you fell into the pond, on the other side of the hill."

The little girl. My mouse demon.

"Brenna? Where is she?" I try to sit up.

"Shhh." Sabine pushes me back down as if I weighed nothing. She sits back on her heels and looks over her shoulder.

Brenna is sitting in a chair beside a raised hearth, hands folded on her lap, watching. Her lips are pressed together as if her mouth has been sewn shut.

"She has been here all this time. I told her she must stop her chattering, for it disturbed your sleep."

At that Brenna comes and sits beside my daughter on the floor. I look past them, at the hearth. It is an oven.

Then I understand. I am in the kitchens of the convent where Brenna and I begged food once, however many days ago. She tied me to a length of trapper's rope and led me here as my mind burned with fever.

"She told me how you have been searching for me," Sabine murmurs, looking down at the plain white front of her gown. She flushes. "It was wrong of me to run off."

I can only shake my head. No, it was not so wrong. Had she stayed, likely she would be in a grave now with her mother. And what of Brenna, had I not found her as I followed the plaguewalker in my dreams? She would have frozen or starved to death.

Then I consider the little mouse demon's resourcefulness. Perhaps I am wrong that it was she who needed me.

I look past Sabine and smile at Brenna's homely features. A man could not want a better child.

The old nun moves away from me. She speaks over her shoulder, to Sabine. "See that he is comfortable, but be sure you are not late for Prime."

I stare at my daughter. "You have taken the veil?"

"Not yet," she says. She looks older. Not a girl anymore. "But I will. It is better than my other options."

As she speaks, her sage-colored eyes avoid mine. A flush like fever advances from the edges of her face. And I understand that she saw much of the world as she traveled from the Scharfrichter's home to here, and found most of it not to her liking.

She glances at the kitchen door, closed now. Her voice lowers to a whisper. "Father, I told them you were a garrison solider. Do not tell them you are a Scharfrichter. They would hold it against me."

I smile at her. I think I am looking at the first nun who has not been baptized.

She need not be anxious. I am not what I was.

Historical Notes

The plague known as the Black Death or Great Dying, which ravaged much of Europe and Asia in the fourteenth century, traveled in two forms.

The better-known bubonic plague was contracted by the bites of infected fleas and killed roughly half of those stricken with it. Recognizable by large black buboes that formed most commonly in the victim's armpits and groin, the bubonic plague struck mostly during warmer months.

The plague was far more deadly in its pneumonic form, however. Occasionally someone with bubonic plague lived long enough for secondary buboes to form in the lungs. Every breath, every sneeze, every cough of this individual unleashed millions of germs. One had only to inhale a single germ to become infected. Once infected with this more virulent strain, the victim was usually dead within 36 hours. The victims of pneumonic plague did not live long enough to manifest the black buboes. Mortality rates for the pneumonic form of plague ranged from 70 to 100 percent. Whole towns were decimated.

Because it killed with such speed, pneumonic plague was not widespread. It would appear suddenly, run its savage course through the local populace, and then disappear.

The Great Dying generated many superstitions. Alleged cures and preventatives ranged from drinking urine to marking clothing and buildings with crosses. Many people in German-speaking regions believed that the plague traveled in the form of Pest Jungfrau, the Plague Maiden, a beautiful young woman in red. People also believed in the Plaguewalker, a black giant who carried the plague on his back.

The executioner, der Scharfrichter, occupied a peculiar place in medieval German society. Reviled by all and forbidden from many of the activities considered essential to the medieval man—such as hunting—he was also considered a mystic who possessed healing powers. The executioner was prohibited from receiving the Sacraments, appearing without his mask in public, conducting commerce, even traveling the main thoroughfares of town. He also typically oversaw the lowest classes of society: supervising the night soil workers and running the local brothel.

The ostracism of the Scharfrichter extended to his family. Wives were often the daughters or sisters of other Scharfrichters, since few women could be induced to marry into a life of restrictions and isolation. It was the right of the Scharfrichter, however, to offer to marry a condemned woman. While some women accepted the proposal, most preferred death.

Most executioners were literate, if only functionally. Along with skills in torture and execution, fathers passed on to sons knowledge of basic medicine, including bone-setting, and herbal remedies. The origin of the knowledge was practical. The executioner had to know how to keep his prisoners alive and healthy enough to confess. But as the lore of the executioners grew, townspeople often sought them out to provide cures or preserved parts of executed criminals believed to have magical powers.

The public execution, often carried out on a Rabenstein (Raven Stone) outside of town, was as much public spectacle as dispensation of justice. Booths selling food and drink were often set up, and large, rowdy crowds gathered as if to witness a sporting event. There are several accounts of crowds beating or even killing a Scharfrichter who failed to perform the difficult act of beheading with a sword to the mob's satisfaction.

About the Author

Gemma Tarlach has been, among other things, a journalist, a diplomat, and a pastry chef. She has lived on four continents and traveled through the other three. Wherever she wanders, writing has been the one constant in her life.

Gemma began researching the story that would ultimately become *Plaguewalker* while living in Bavaria in the early 1990s. It would be the first novel she wrote that was inspired by her travels. She is currently at work on the final draft of a fantasy novel, *The War's End*, and its sequel, *The Guardian*. Like *Plaguewalker*, both novels involve a great deal of walking in the cold, one of her favorite pastimes and the place where she hears her characters best.

Perhaps not coincidentally, Gemma currently lives and works at McMurdo Station, Ross Island, Antarctica. Tales about her experiences there, as well as other travels through the Southern Hemisphere, can be found at *storiesthataretrue.wordpress.com*.

Made in the USA
Lexington, KY
03 July 2012